Dilemma

Mozart's Medicine

By Jerry Bader

ISBN Paperback: 978-1-988647-70-8

Hard Cover: 978-1-988647-71-5

Ebook: 978-1-988647-72-2

The Italian Way

Girolama's black plastic slicker glistens in the multiple-coloured glare of neon, offering exotic delicacies designed to tantalize the hungry tourists that prowl London's Chinatown. The rain slides off her hood as if trying to escape the inevitable. It's an awkward time, a time when the world can't make up its mind whether it is day or night, a time when mortality comes to mind.

She knows the place they are to meet, The Thirsty Dragon, a moderately-priced restaurant frequented by foreign visitors attracted by the kitschy Chinese interior and faded images of food that decorate the facade. Everything about the place is mediocre, not her kind of place. The food, like most western versions of Chinese fare, bears little resemblance to the authentic cuisine. More to the point, her taste favours more high-end alternatives, but the place suited her purpose, unremarkable in every aspect.

Each meeting is at a different location. Avoid patterns at all costs, that is what they told her and that is what she does. She knows better than to freelance. The Thirsty Dragon is perfect, a tourist trap where repeat diners are uncommon. Even if people do come back for a rerun of second rate cooking, the sullen, preoccupied imported Hong Kong staff wouldn't remember them. They don't give a damn, an attitude that seems to dominate relationships with outsiders. If you've ever done business with the Chinese, you know what I mean. I once went to a Chinese restaurant with a woman who was allergic to seafood. She explained the problem in great detail to the waiter who nodded solicitously as she spoke. He promised to inform the kitchen whose staff decided the solution to the problem was chopping the seafood up into small pieces so my friend didn't realize she was eating shrimp. I had to rush her to the hospital later that night, but I digress. By now, you should be used to my excursions into irrelevancy, as this is the third of such reports I've submitted.

Girolama liked Jimmy, but her father made it clear, he had to go. The software he provided contained the Mozart malware, an upgrade to the older PoisonIvy version, a virus that functions as a remote access trojan giving the infiltrators the ability to record or manipulate content including a device's audio and camera functions.

No one knew exactly how much damage it caused or what secrets were divulged, but the incident meant heads would roll. The virtual hole in the dike was eventually plugged, they hoped.

There is always the chance that Mozart was a misdirection and some other malware was still worming its way through their telecommunication systems.

It's possible Jimmy didn't know, but somebody knew. Ether Jimmy was working for British intelligence or somebody he worked with did. They knew there was a leak and used Jimmy Cotton to plug it, and now Jimmy was going to pay the ultimate price.

Girolama spots Jimmy in a banquette in the dimly lit back corner of the restaurant as he was instructed. He's nursing a glass of house red while nervously stacking and unstacking packets of sweetener. A Yorkie chocolate bar sits untouched but open in front of him. Girolama slides into the faux leather bench leaving her raincoat on with the excuse her jeans and sweatshirt are covered in paint. The rain from the hood of her slicker drips onto her face. She is attractive in an exotic, offbeat arty way.

"You look like shit."

"I haven't been feeling well lately. You want this chocolate bar, the sight of it is making me sick?"

"I can't eat that. I'm allergic to chocolate." She pauses, "Did you bring it?" He reaches under the table and taps Girolama's knee with the new thumb drive. She takes the drive and slides it into her coat pocket." This drive would be reverse-engineered and destroyed. It would never get close to their telecommunications network.

"Go throw some cold water on your face before you puke all over me."

He hesitates, "All right." He takes a big gulp of his wine, gets up, and heads for the bathroom.

The slicker's hood covers Girolama's face but she still looks around to make sure no one is eyeing her. If Jimmy is working for MI5 he might have a partner and even if he doesn't, they still might be tailing him. Everything looks normal. She takes a small flacon out of her pocket. She removes the cap and dumps the contents into the wine glass. She takes a paper napkin in her hand, wraps it around the stem of the glass, and swirls the wine around until the powder dissolves. Jimmy returns to the table and sits, He doesn't look any better. "You still look pale, drink some more wine." Jimmy takes a sip.

"You can do better than that. Take a drink like a man. Put some colour back in your cheeks." He does what he's told and finishes the rest of the poisoned red wine.

"Good." She gets up to leave.

"Where are you going? I thought we'd go back to my place and… you know…" His voice trails off in a half-hearted effort to lure her back to his flat.

"Not tonight, Jimmy, besides you look like you need your rest. Go home, get into bed, and sleep. I'll make contact in a few days." She doesn't wait for a reply. She adjusts the hood of the slicker making sure it covers her face. She leaves.

Three days later, Jimmy's cleaning lady, Maria McGill, arrives at his front door to find his flat swarming with people. Two policemen guard the open front door. Inside a chubby young man with a remarkable resemblance to Jack Black is pulling things out of Jimmy's desk. On the other side of the room, a woman who looks like she's late for her kid's soccer practice is going through Jimmy's bookshelves, rifling through volumes in what looks like an attempt to find hidden messages. In the middle of the room, four people stand arguing, Roger Ames and Kevin Mark of MI6 on one side with Charlie Thompson and Melinda Byrnes of MI5 on the other. The discussion is heated.

Ames spots the woman waiting at the door. He looks at Byrnes, "Find out who she is and get rid of her." Byrnes looks at Thompson, unsure of exactly who she's supposed to take orders from. Ames notices the hesitation, "Your ID may say MI5 but you work for me now. Get rid of her."

Byrnes goes to the door, shows Maria her ID, and asks her who she is. Maria tells her she's Jimmy's cleaning lady. "When was the last time you saw Mr. Cotton?"

"Last week, when I came to clean. He didn't look well. Is he okay?"

"Mr. Cotton no longer needs your services."

"I'm fired? What did I do?"

"You didn't do anything. Jimmy Cotton is dead."

Eventually, the coroner finds no evidence of foul play. Software engineer, Jimmy Cotton's murder is ruled death by natural causes. Roger Ames and Charlie Thompson know better. The untimely demise of Jimmy Cotton is just the beginning of Mozart's revenge.

D.O.A.

He sits down across from me and places his briefcase under the table. He looks so average you might easily mistake him for one of those police composite sketches. There is nothing about him that stands out. He is one of those people that are instantly forgettable. He had all the qualities of a ghost or perhaps a spy; the difference may not be a difference. I know the term spy has gone out of fashion, replaced by more mundane nebulous terms, that like the job itself seems to evaporate before your eyes, but then he opened his mouth, "They killed me." His accent suggests he's American.

Was this another of my deluded episodes, another mental movie running a rehashed remake of the classic 1949 noir thriller, D.O.A.? The image of Edmond O'Brien marching into police headquarters to announce his own demise exploded across my brain like a train-wreck about to engulf me one more time. Was I back in play? Was Roger behind this meeting? Would Harriet suddenly appear?

The agency cut me loose, but Roger made it clear I was still under his pedantic thumb. He'd left me alone for six months, my reward for moving Arno

Koch to the cutting floor of existence. I'm at peace with what I've done, after all, the man was a pharmacological Josef Mengele, an all-around creep. Read the report, it's all there in black and white. Perhaps my former Vauxhall Cross masters shredded the paper trail, but you know the story, all of it, in vivid surround-sound technicolor detail.

Since my resurrection as the nondescript art dealer known as Harry Rasske, I live quietly in my third-floor loft, painting abstract messes on canvas. I kill time checking on my investment in the restaurant and jazz club I rescued from bankruptcy and running the adjacent London Bowley Art Gallery in a renovated ironworks factory that serves as my headquarters. If a cover story was intended, it is a good one.

Mercury, the woman, not the chemical element is my partner in both the Toronto gallery and the London version. Since we last communicated Mercury and I have become a thing, despite the annoyance of the all too frequent international travel. In case you're wondering I did tell her about Harriet, to which she just smiled and kissed me on the forehead. Her only response was "Everyone has their fantasies, Harry. Mine is Horst Janssen." We both laughed at the idea of the beautiful Mercury and the pudgy German.

As you are aware, this is not the first time a stranger sat down at my table and demanded my attention. You may remember Harriet's entrance into my mental movie, but then how could you forget the female *force majeure*. But this new player in my drama had none of the qualities that Harriet used to ignite my hidden desires.

This shadow of a man wasn't nearly as interesting as my occasional sidekick, but then as we've discussed before, the lovely Harriet may not actually exist; she may merely be an imaginative invention of my overly active noggin. But I have to admit I was interested. The *Sister Project* and the *Lucy's Breath* businesses had awakened something in me that demanded to be served. A need to act and not just stand by and watch as the world disintegrates into a vile authoritarian compost of madness.

Perhaps Roger recognized that aspect of my personality and thus, directed me on my rather unsanctioned journey of fulfillment. I'd come to accept Roger as someone I had to deal with despite the fact I wasn't all that convinced he played by the rules. But of course, our business has no real rules, just paper pretences to protect the politicians from taking ownership of the meanings hidden between the lines of their creatively vague, yet deceptively clear intents. Roger is one such creature, someone who lives between the lines, between the words and the meaning, but enough of this preamble. The man in front of me claims he's been murdered, and I suppose he wants me to do something about it.

I make a stab of putting the poor soul off. "This is obviously a police matter. I'm just an art dealer, not a policeman." It came out sounding like Scotty responding to Captain Kirk, claiming the warp drive can't be fixed, *it's impossible, Captain, I'll have it done in an hour.*

"Roger sent me. He said you'd find who killed me. He said you were good at snooping."

That certainly sounds like Roger. And if Roger is involved, this isn't just a matter of murder. This must have international implications, national security must be in the mix. Anything domestic falls under MI5's watchful eyes, thus my unofficial status becomes useful to the Circus ringmasters of Vauxhall Cross.

My new friend did not look well. He kept clutching his stomach as if in pain. He looked green, giving the appearance he was working hard not to spill his lunch all over my neighbourhood café's freshly laundered table linen. He kept glancing out the window as if he expected someone or something. "I'm being followed. The red Land Rover across the street."

His claim gives me doubts. "Professionals don't use bright red SUV's to tail people."

"They do if they want you to know they're there."

He had a point. The question is why? "Why would someone want you dead? And why would they want you to know?"

"I'm sorry... I thought I lost them on the Tube. I've led them straight to you. I better leave before they get suspicious. Be careful. They killed me. They'll kill you too if you're not smart, but Roger says you're clever. You better be if you want to survive. Everything you need is in the briefcase." He pushes the case towards me with his foot.

He gets up from the table and leaves the café. I follow him with my eyes. He stands on the corner, waiting for an opening in the traffic so he can cross the street.

He looks the wrong way as Americans are ought to do in Britain. He steps off the curb heading straight for the red Land Rover. There's a squeal of tires and a loud bang; an oncoming grey Mini

Cooper veers onto the sidewalk striking my new friend throwing him into and through the window of the café. His body sprawls akimbo on the floor of the restaurant. The grey Mini never stops. It swerves back onto the road and speeds off down the busy street. I'm able to catch the first three letters of the license plate, 1-3-5. I scribble them on a scrap of paper from the notebook I always carry in my jacket pocket. The red Land Rover starts its engine and drives off.

My table is covered in glass. I feel pain. There is something wet and gooey on my forehead. I touch my temple. I'm bleeding where the glass from the window decided to use my head as a backstop. I pick up the briefcase and leave.

The Briefcase

I sit in my Bauhaus retreat staring at the George Condo hanging on the wall. I like Condo's work. It's strange and intelligent in its Picasso-esk style, turning human beings inside-out so that their inner reality blasts you in the face like a beloved Mickey Mouse telling you to *fuck off*.

I get it, like Condo, I see the puddle of deceit, envy, and intellectual corruption that spills out from the carefully coiffed creatures that occupy this planet. That may sound arrogant and elitist, but I only admit to the latter, as the former requires far too much self-confidence from its adherents for me to be associated.

My eyes go to the briefcase that lies open on the freeform bronze and glass sculpture that passes for my coffee table. There are files, a used wine glass still stained with red, and two keys. One is a safe deposit box key from Barclays Bank on Vauxhall Bridge Rd and the other could be a key to his flat. Attached to the keys is a tag labelled D. D. Greyson Notting Hill, 1023 Portobello Road, Unit 3. I assume it's the address of my D.O.A.

The files contain research from some website easily conjured with a simple click of a mouse.

The notes describe various exotic poisons used to kill. Most have fallen out of favour as a mere dose of high-performance opioids will do the trick. It seems the most likely delivery system based on the fact we live in a society of diluted nincompoops that think it's their god-given right to feel good all the time. It's not surprising the authorities pay little or no attention to self-medicated dopes. Just another fool chasing an elusive nirvana. And so, my D.O.A.'s killers figured nobody would notice his slow departure from our shared earthly precinct, but something changed their plans. Slow and easy wouldn't work for his executioners. Immediate and deadly action was called for, thus the swerving grey Mini Cooper makes its dramatic entrance leaving me with a stained wine glass in one hand, a safe deposit key in the other, and a Roger-induced pain in my ass.

But Greyson genuinely thought he was being poisoned and that was my best lead. The list he made includes Hemlock or Conium, the classic Greek toxin of Socrates' fame. According to the notes, 100mg or eight leaves from the source plant will do the job. Another plant used for *offing* friends and family is Wolfsbane or Aconite, a derivative of the monkshood plant that can cause asphyxia from a mere touch.

Other killer substances researched by the recently dispatched, D. D. Greyson, are Belladonna, the favourite of disillusioned seventeenth-century Italian wives, Dimethylmercury, a slow-acting manmade killer, Tetrodotoxin, produced by an irritated blue-ringed octopus, and Polonium, the radioactive instrument of death used by a couple of Russians to kill the former FSB Colonel, Alexander Litvinenko. This one was of special interest to me, as it was used to murder a traitorous spy. The fact that I was sitting across from a potentially radio-active time-bomb did not augur well for my own good health.

Other substances researched by Greyson included Mercury, the chemical element, not my partner in business and pleasure, along with Cyanide, Botulinum, and everyone's favourite, Arsenic.

What Greyson left off his list was grey Mini Coopers, the ultimate vehicle that delivered the final death blow, but was the reinvented Mini merely the *coup de grâce?* He knew he was a dead man walking. He said, "They killed me." not "They're going to kill me." He believed he was poisoned and his appearance certainly seemed to corroborate that suspicion. The fact he kept the stained wine glass as evidence indicates he already guessed what was happening to him. The glass could prove he was poisoned. And if there were someone else's fingerprints on it, it might even lead to the murderer.

I could ignore the whole thing but we both know that wasn't going to happen. I am hooked. Perhaps I need the adrenaline rush, the excitement of the hunt, or perhaps I miss Harriet who seems to appear out of nowhere whenever I get in trouble. First, I had to contact Roger to find out what he knew and what he expected me to do. Second, I needed to get the wine glass analyzed, Roger could help with that. And finally, a trip to Barclays seemed to be in order.

Would the lovely Harriet make an appearance to help guide me through this operation, or has she evaporated into thin air like the ghost she seems to be. Perhaps my relationship with Mercury has exorcized Harriet from my world.

The Roger Factor

I check in with Billy who runs the London Bowley for me. You may remember Billy, Mercury's assistant in the Toronto gallery. Together Mercury and Billy do all the work, I merely hang around to take the credit and pay the bills. After a brief discussion of housekeeping issues, Billy hands me an envelope. "It came first thing this morning."

I open the envelope. It's a ticket to tonight's performance featuring Mozart's Concerto No. 3 "Adagio" performed by the London Symphony Orchestra at the Barbican Hall on Silk Street.

There's a note that simply reads, "*See you there, lover. - H*" I will admit to a quickening of my pulse and a flash of guilt that prompts me to call Mercury. "Hi, it's me."

"I recognize the voice, but don't seem to be able to attach a face."

"I know, I miss you too."

"Is something wrong; have you got yourself involved in another of your," she pauses searching for just the right word, "adventures?"

"Something like that."

"Has your Harriet made an appearance?"

"Tonight, at the theatre, she sent the ticket."

"A rendezvous, how romantic, I'm jealous."

"Don't be, somebody was murdered."

"Oh... perhaps that Roger friend of yours."

"No, not Roger, and he's no friend, just an associate of sorts."

"Be careful Harry, I like you a lot, and would weep if anything dramatic happened to you."

"I like you a lot as well."

"How's Billy doing in the land of afternoon tea and biscuits?"

"Great, between you and Billy, my job seems to be just staying out of the way."

She laughs, "True, but still, it's nice to have you around."

"As soon as this current business is wrapped up, I'll come home. Billy can handle everything here. He even keeps an eye on the nightclub for me, he's becoming a real player around here."

"That will be nice. Just be careful and say hello to Harriet for me."

"Sure, and you to Horst."

"You know he's dead."

"I do, but Harriet may be real."

"What if Harriet wasn't the one that sent you the ticket?"

"I guess I'll find out tonight."

"Be very careful, Harry, no more Chinese horse paintings, please?"

"I'll do my best. You know I love you."

"And I, you, *Chao.*"

After we hang up, I head for my meeting with Roger, my ex-gaffer at the agency and my current occasional employer. Roger's latest job is running a task-force of cyber boffins and black op stringers tasked with protecting the country from foreign meddling. The problem is, anything domestic is MI5 business, not the Circus, but of course, the two intelligence services rarely see eye-to-eye on matters of jurisdiction or trust. And so, the Quandary Research Organization was created as a front to do things my former agency was technically forbidden to do.

I didn't mention to Roger what the meeting was about, but since he sent Greyson to me, I assumed he would know. We agreed to meet at the Bull and Peacock, a local pub near where the late D. D. Greyson ended his onscreen performance. I spot Roger alone at a table in the back of the pub.

It seemed appropriate that Roger, the Peacock fop, would find a comfortable spot in the arse-end of the Bull. As you may surmise, Roger and I are not mates. I don't trust him and never have. He may not be the Kim Philby clone I first suspected, but the bastard would flush me down the crapper of life faster than a bad case of diarrhea.

He greets me with his usual condescending bravado, "Well hello, old chap, it's been a donkey's age. Enjoying my Graf von Faber-Castell." The reference requires a long explanation and not important at this time. If you insist on knowing the details, you can refer to my previous lengthy memos that deal with the fountain pen issue extensively. I ignore the taunt, I'm keeping the fucking pen.

"Roger..."

"So dear boy, what can I do for you? Bored dealing with rich fools willing to drop the price of a Kensington flat for one of those drippy musings you sell in your gallery? No? But you are looking for work. Oh my, you haven't gone through your late Uncle's fortune, have you, spent on your incomprehensible fascination with the abstract doodlings of your bohemian pals?"

"No Roger, my business interests are quite profitable and more than pay for my interest in abstract expressionism."

"So then, what can I do for you?"

"D. D. Greyson, what's the story?"

"I'm sorry, Harry, I don't know what you're talking about."

"Really? You didn't send some shadow of a man to see me because he thought someone had killed him?"

"Seems you're not the only one with an overripe imagination. or is this another of your fantasies? Seen Harriet lately?"

"Don't be a *knob*, Roger, who the hell is D. D. Greyson and why the hell did someone kill him?"

Roger suddenly becomes serious, dropping the old boy bullshit. "I'm confused, Harry, what's this all about?"

I tell Roger the story from the beginning: how Greyson approached me at the café; that he thought someone was poisoning him; that he was being followed by a Land Rover; and that he was struck and killed while crossing the street.

"This seems like a local police matter, Harry. Let them handled it."

"I don't think so, Roger. Something is going on. Why would Greyson say, you of all people, sent him to me? When his followers saw him with me, they decided they couldn't wait for the poison to take effect. Someone sent him to us for a reason and I'll bet you a Kensington flat's worth of abstraction that this is a security issue."

"How can I help?"

"I need you to analyze the wine glass he gave me to see if he was really poisoned as he thought. I couldn't find anything online for a D. D. Greyson so I assume that was some kind of alias. There should be fingerprints or DNA on the glass. See what you can dig up on this guy. I was able to catch the first three numbers on the Mini Cooper, 1-3-5, see if that rings any bells?"

"Did you say 1-3-5?"

"Yes."

"That's a Chinese diplomatic plate. I'm afraid you're right, this is interesting. Someone is sending us a signal. Whatever the Chinese are doing, someone wants us to stop it. "

"Who?"

"Know any Chinese diplomats that don't always go along with the party line."

"I know one."

"Yeah, so do I, Yang Guozhi, chief muckety-muck of the Economic Division of the Ministry of State Security."

"Did you get the plate of the red Land Rover?"

A mistake, I specifically didn't tell him the Land Rover was red. Roger Ames, the ultra-professional intelligence officer just fucked-up. I don't let on. The error most certainly has significance and is bound to come into play.

"Sorry, no. It was across the street. I didn't get a good angle. Whoever it was, was careful." Of course they were careful, it was Roger's people. Exactly what the hell is going on? Roger did send Greyson to me. He was probably told not to tell me it was Roger, but he was in such a bad state, he forgot, or just didn't care. He knew he was a deadman and protecting Roger was the last thing on his mind. Roger seems intent on messing with me, perhaps because he knows I think he could be a double, or maybe he feels I put his wink-and-nod counterintelligence operation in danger, or maybe he wants me dead because I took his fucking expensive fountain pen.

"Too bad," The slight quiver of his stiff upper lip betrays his relief. He thinks I missed the tell, but I too have become professional, leaving my amateur status behind in that utility closet in the basement of the Toronto Consulate.

It wouldn't be a stretch for Roger to have Greyson killed with a car carrying Chinese diplomatic plates. I did not like the direction this operation was taking. Roger and I had a history. The fact that we were moderately civil to one another did not hide the intense distrust I had for him and the complete absence of loyalty he had for me. As far as Roger was concerned, I was his go-to patsy for operations that could, and probably would, go wrong.

The Salieri Conspiracy

I arrive at Barbican Hall ten minutes before the concert is scheduled to start. My ticket is for an aisle seat. The concert hall is full except for the seat beside me that remains empty. The lights dim while the orchestra warms up. I continuously check my watch. I'm nervous. I haven't seen the beautiful Harriet since that business in Washington with Yang Guozhi and the Chinese ink horse paintings.

I feel someone tap me on the shoulder. It's Harriet. "Move over, Harry dear, I'll take the aisle." She kisses me on the cheek and squeezes my hand. "And how is the lovely Mercury, my rival in love?"

I don't know what to say, but she does. "It's okay, my love, I do understand. We both know I just can't be your Mercury, but I do remain your Harriet." She pauses in her usual dramatic style, she will always be the Bacall to my Bogart. "Poor Harry, the man with two lovers, it's such a dilemma, but don't fret, two things in conflict can both be true. Something you should keep in mind. It is the spy's dilemma."

I feel like a schoolboy on a first date. She squeezes my hand one more time. She moves to get up, "Come, Harry, Mozart will have to do without our presence. We have things to discuss."

We leave the concert hall and head for a nearby pub. Harriet takes my arm as we walk along the artificial waterway that fronts the concert hall. I know we'll never make it to the pub.

"You want to tell me what's going on with Roger and this D.D. Greyson business?"

"To be frank, I'm not supposed to tell you anything, but I can at least point you in a direction."

"Are you working for Roger and his illegal *ad hoc* enterprise?"

"Legal, illegal, sanctioned, unsanctioned, in our business, the difference isn't a difference. All that matters is we don't get caught." You notice she didn't answer the question.

"And what exactly am I supposed to not get caught doing, or is Roger just setting me up to take the fall for some nasty business he's involved in?"

"Perhaps you shouldn't have stolen his pen."

"Jesus... Roger and his fucking pen, I didn't steal it, I just took it from him."

"Potato, po-tah-to, tomato, to-mah-to, like I said, is there a difference?"

"Fuck him. I'm keeping the pen."

"Let's move on, shall we. The pen is hardly the issue. If Roger wants you dead, or merely the fall guy for one of his operations, then it's important to keep your eye on the ball."

"Okay fine, but I don't know what I'm doing."

"I can tell you this, D. D. Greyson was an accountant, investment councillor, and venture capitalist. A one-man Mossack Fonseca but with national security implications. Find out what he was into and follow the money."

"I'm no financial expert. Why me?"

"You're a rich man, Harry, you know about money and you travel in the right circles. Besides, your expertise in the art business is why it's you."

"That doesn't make sense, Harriet, I run a little art gallery. My clients aren't threats."

"Not so little, Harry." She stops walking, kisses me with her usual enthusiasm and extracts her arm from mine. "You know some think Salieri poisoned Mozart. Mozart's Medicine I call it, Italian revenge, fit for a political rival. It's not true of course, but then what is truth anyway, the Americans seem to have murdered that concept all by themselves. But the notion of death for political chicanery still has the smell of truth, and all art is political in one way or another."

"That's a bit of a *non sequitur* isn't it?"

'Is it? Maybe it is. Maybe it isn't. Follow the breadcrumbs, Harry, you never know what you'll find." I watch as she starts walking away.

"Harriet…" she turns, "when will I see you again?"

"We might run into one another at the Expo. You never know. You're on the right path, Harry, the breadcrumbs will point you in the direction you need to go." She turns the corner and disappears into the night.

Greyson's Box

The following morning I head for Barclay's to re-trieve the contents of Greyson's safe deposit box. The box contains another key to what appears to be a storage locker as well as two ledgers. One account book contains a sales journal with client names, product numbers, and sales figures; the other is a supplier's journal with just two names, Girolama Spera and the 798 Art Frame Company, but a lengthy list of product numbers and pur-chase figures.

Whatever Greyson was buying and selling, the net seemed to be extremely profitable. He ap-peared to be arranging loans for clients from the Enterprise Bank of China for small amounts of between a thousand and two thousand pounds. The money was used to purchase items for these clients from Spera. Greyson then resold the mys-tery items for inflated prices ranging from ten to fifteen thousand pounds to companies with Chi-nese names or connections. Greyson pocketed roughly thirty percent of the final sale price while his client received the rest. My first im-pression was Greyson was running a drug money laundering operation. Murder is often the ulti-mate exit strategy for drug dealers. That would explain Greyson's hit and run.

It also wouldn't surprise me that Roger would be neck-deep in a drug-money-laundering business to finance his unsanctioned Quandary Research outfit, but why the Chinese connection. I know from the *Lucy's Breath* business that there is significant bureaucratic infighting within the Ministry of State Security. Certain groups are intent on corrupting Western morals by facilitating the export of drugs to the West, while my old enemy, Yang Guozhi of the Enterprise Division, is more interested in selling Chinese merchandise rather than turning British dopes into dopers.

Roger and Yang are far too cozy for my good health. The pair already set me up for the Pijiu murder in Washington last year, a murder I didn't commit but one that cost me my name and career, forcing me to leave Toronto, change my identity and rid the world of Arno Koch. It was the price I was forced to pay in order to get the Americans and Interpol off my back. This whole deal smelled a lot like a rerun. The wildcard in this mess is Girolama Spera.

Follow the breadcrumbs, that's what Harriet said, and that is exactly what I intend to do. Next on the agenda is a visit to City Storage Company on Peerless Road, Unit 1089. Hopefully, I'll find more crumbs to follow.

The Storage Locker

I left my vintage '54 MG back in Toronto with in-structions that Mercury could drive it, but only in good weather, as Toronto winters demanded a heartier vehicle to traverse the almost impossible traffic and foul weather. Without my prized baby available, I felt I needed a lift, something indulgent without being ostentatious. A black Alfa Romeo Spider with camel leather interior was the answer. Running around London searching for clues wasn't the best way to break-in my new roadster but maybe this operation would eventually give me a chance to turn my new ride loose on the open motorway.

Before I go to the storage facility, I stop off at an old-style hardware store to buy a couple of high-end locks. I have the feeling they'll come in handy. The owner of the shop assures me these new ultra-expensive locks are unbreakable. I'm skeptical but figure I'd give them a try. Who knows who else has access to the unit.

As I leave the hardware store I spot a red Land Rover SUV parked down the street. I do my best to pretend I don't spot it. I'm being tailed, but the question is, by who? Is it the Chinese, Roger, or someone else?

If it's the Chinese, is it Yang's people looking to protect the People's commercial interests, or is it the Little Red Book ideologues looking to further disrupt the already decadent morals of Western libertines. Perhaps it's Roger and his unsanctioned Quandary cabal, after all, he feigned not knowing Greyson or anything he was doing, but he still knew the colour of the Land Rover without me telling him. Maybe it's someone else at MI6, a stickler for the rules, that doesn't like the idea of Roger's little band of spies meddling in domestic business. It may even be MI5 looking to put a rogue MI6 operative in the slammer for horning in on their business.

Whoever it is, I have to lose them, or at least put them off my trail with some misdirection. Instead of going directly to the storage unit I take a circuitous route around downtown London, ending up at the Chelsea Retreat where I decide to have lunch. While finishing my Cobb Salad I phone Billy and tell him I'm on my way back to the gallery. I tell him to go up to my flat and get the Beretta I keep in the bedside night table and to wait for me there.

When I get home, Billy and I exchange clothes. I secure the Beretta in a leather shoulder holster under Billy's blazer. I look at the two of us in the full-length mirror on the inside of my walk-in closet. Since we are both about the same size, it will be hard to tell Billy isn't me, especially if you're sitting in a red Land Rover trying not to be spotted. I give him my car keys and tell him to visit half-a-dozen storage facilities and rent units under the name, D. D. Greyson. I look up storage units on Google and designate which ones I want Billy to use.

"This could be dangerous and definitely not part of your job. You don't have to do this."

"Are you kidding? I'm in."

"Okay, but be careful. Make sure the red Land Rover is following you and knows where you're going. Keep them as far away from the City Storage Company as possible. Spend at least fifteen minutes in each unit so they think you're doing something. Do your best not to let them see your face. When you're done come back here, change clothes and act normal."

We leave the gallery parking lot at the same time with Billy in my car and clothes heading in one direction and me in the van and Billy's clothes heading in the other.

I find the City Storage facility without much trouble. I go to the office and rent a new unit under a false name as far away from Greyson's as possible. I pull Billy's van up to Greyson's unit and enter. The unit is filled with colourful paintings reminiscent of the late Richard Lindner's work. Lindner was a cult figure of pop art fame and his paintings are extraordinary. These attempts, in my opinion, are good without being great. The artist did his or her best to capture the grotesque eroticism of the sexes that Lindner seemed to revel in, but this artist's work lacked Lindner's originality and bizarre flamboyance.

It seemed clear there was more to this endeavour than maintaining artistic integrity. The paintings were large, colourful, and decorative with just enough sexual energy to be thought of as art by those who needed something to match their sofa. The real purpose of these creations would be found not in the world of art but rather in the world of commerce.

Don't get me wrong, much of art, if not most, is transactional rather than transformative, but the same can be said about the business of espionage. Although there are those pure of heart, ideologues that would lay down their lives for the cause, the truth is, the vast majority of what passes for covert patriotism is merely transactional; money for information, even if it's worthless. Everything has a price. Of course, I can be cynical about these matters because I'm rich and can afford to be a true patriot with the foreknowledge that everyone else is corrupt, or at least, corruptible.

There's a large cabinet in the back of the unit with the kind of cheap lock used by schoolboys to hide their pornography. I find a hammer left there for no apparent reason and use it to smash the lock. I'm not surprised when I open the cabinet. It's stuffed with neat stacks of twenty-pound notes. Each bundle of currency is labelled two-thousand pounds and piled neatly in twelve rows that almost come up to my knees.

It is a lot of money, maybe as much as one million quid. It's a good thing I bought the new locks. I back the van into the unit and fill it with the paintings. The cabinet with the cash is too heavy to move so instead I dump the money into two green garbage bags Billy left in the back of the van. I lock the unit with one of my new locks.

I drive to the new unit and unload the paintings and the two green garbage bags. I pick one of the better paintings and put it back in the van. I attach another new lock to the door of the storage room and head back to the gallery.

On my way back to the flat, I get a call on my mobile from Roger. He has information and wants to meet. I tell him I'll be at the Bull and Peacock in an hour. I call Billy who tells me he's on his way back to the gallery and that the Land Rover has stuck to him like a *Fritessaus* on chips.

When I get back to the gallery, Billy and I exchange clothes and car keys. I take the key to Greyson's safe deposit box stick it in an envelope and address it to myself with the Toronto gallery as the return address. I take the key to the storage unit and stick it in a second envelope and address it to the Toronto mailbox I set up for just such a purpose. I enclose a note to Mercury, the only other person that has access to the mailbox, telling her to keep the key in a safe place. I drop the envelopes into the mailbox in front of the gallery and head for the Bull and Peacock.

The Conversation

When I get to the Bull and Peacock, Roger is already there nursing a pint. I take a seat across the table. Roger takes a sip of his room temperature ale. "Want a pint, old chap?"

"No thanks, I don't drink beer."

"And you say I'm a snob."

I ignore the crack, even though the implication is true, I am a snob, at least about some things. Being half-British and half-Canadian, you'd think any fermented barley swill would be high on my list of must-have food groups, but the fact is, I never developed a taste for it. If I have to drink, I'll stick to a Vodka Collins.

"You had something to tell me?"

"Greyson... he was an accountant of sorts."

Roger doesn't know Harriet already told me this, which could lead you to believe she exists. And to be honest, I am leaning in that direction. However, the brain is an inscrutable device and Harriet may merely be my way of figuring things out. Then again, there is the way she kisses me, often leaving a trickle of blood on my lip as a remembrance. Of course, the blood could also be caused by me absentmindedly biting my lip.

"What do you mean of sorts."

"He was involved with some woman, an artist, Girolama Spera, perhaps he was using her artwork to launder money? It's quite common in your racket, as I'm sure you already know. Maybe that's why he came to you."

"So you think he was killed by some mobster because they caught him skimming?"

"Sure, that's probably it, not my business. I don't get involved in local police matters. If there aren't any national security implications I move on."

I couldn't tell if Roger was playing me or he was dismissing the whole matter as beyond the scope of his brief. If he knows as much as he's telling me, he also knows Yang's Enterprise Bank of China is involved. And if Yang is involved, Roger is interested.

Maybe this goes deeper than I originally thought. It appears Roger wants to shut it down, but he also wants to protect his Quandary people from any unfortunate Whitehall blowback or ruffled

MI5 feathers. Thus, I become an expendable in-
dependent contractor. Or, I could merely serve as
an escape valve if things go wrong with his very
own Hole-In-A-Wall Gang. By keeping the paintings and the cash, not to mention Greyson's
ledgers, I might be playing right into his plan to
hang me out to dry, but as the saying goes, *in for
a penny, in for a royal fucking.*

"I think I'll continue to investigate."

"Well, if you insist. You will let me know what
you find out? I am curious, you never know
where things lead."

"Sure, Roger, of course. You know me, always
willing to help the nation in its hour of need. By
the way, did you get the results from Greyson's
wine glass?"

"Yes, actually I did, more proof that this is a police matter rather than a national security one."

"So what did you find?"

"The glass contained residue of wine, lead, arsenic, and belladonna. Police autopsy records
confirm the findings. He was definitely poisoned
despite what the corner's report says. Someone

wanted him dead, but for some reason couldn't wait for the poison to work."

"That's an odd way to poison someone, isn't it?"

"I suppose. Poison is generally used by women, men are by nature more direct."

"I could use some official status. It would help open some doors."

"That's a bit of a problem, old boy, as my little band of brothers isn't exactly kosher itself, that said, I did bring you a present. Something to help you turn the screws on that artist woman. As I said, poison is a woman's weapon, and the combination of ingredients has a definite Italian flair about it."

"I can't wait."

Roger takes a brown eight-and-a-half-by-eleven envelope from the seat beside him and slides it across the table.

"What's this?"

"It may not be official or particularly legal, but it will do the job."

I open the package. It contains a British passport, driver's license and police identification with my picture. Each item lists H. Caul as the owner. The police ID identifies me as a DCI, Detective Chief Inspector. I smile.

"Do you like your rank?"

"I like the name even better?

"I thought you would, after all, you do like old movies, and you are so good at snooping. Just what this matter needs."

"Thanks, Roger, I think?"

I leave Roger and head back to my car. I have to think. Roger's reference to 'an Italian flair' obviously points a finger at Spera as the one who poisoned Greyson, that is, unless he's sending me on some wild goose chase while his people follow the real evidence. Perhaps I'm supposed to be the misdirection leading the red SUV around in circles. I wouldn't put it past him.

I enter lead, arsenic and belladonna into Google on my phone to see what comes up. My eyes glance up at the sideview-mirror. Half a block down and across the street is a red Land Rover.

I call Billy. "London Bowley, William Boyd, Gallery Director."

"Billy, it's me."

"What's up boss, what do you need?"

"I need you to rent me a car, something innocuous, you know, something a red Land Rover wouldn't mistake for a Spider."

"No problem."

"Take it around the corner from the gallery and wait for me." We hang up.

I need to give Billy time to arrange for the car rental. In the meantime, I check to see what Google found regarding the ingredients of the poison. The results are interesting and seem to confirm the involvement of the artist. Lead, arsenic and belladonna are what's known as *Aqua Tofana*, the favourite poison of seventeenth-century mass-murderer, Giulia Tofana.

The concoction was sold as a cosmetic blusher under the name *Manna di San Nicola* in vials with a picture of St. Nicholas. Although some women used it for cosmetic purposes, its main intent was to rid unhappy wives of their less than desirable spouses.

Giulia Tofana had a thriving cosmetic and murder-for-hire business until she was caught and executed along with her daughter known as the *Astrologa della Lungara,* but her actual name was Girolama Spera. It seems Harriet was also pointing me in Spera's direction with her reference to the conspiracy theory accusing Antonio Salieri of poisoning Mozart with *Aqua Tofana.* It seems all the breadcrumbs lead to the artist.

I meander my way around downtown London until I finally lose the red Land Rover. I meet-up with Billy and we switch cars.

The Artist's Lair

I still haven't been to Greyson's flat, so that's my next stop. I doubt I'll find anything new but it's always best to be thorough. It would be stupid of Greyson to keep any incriminating evidence in his residence. He had the safe deposit box and storage unit for that kind of thing.

In my brief time as an unsanctioned field agent, I've learned that you can never overestimate the criminal mind, and I suppose, that applies to traitors as well. They often spend more time and effort in their clandestine machinations than would be required by a more legitimate approach to achieve the same end. People make mistakes or they just get sloppy; it's human nature. As you can tell, I have as little faith in mankind as I do in myself. We are a morass of deception, delusion, and contradictions, and quite frankly, intensely stupid, look who we elect to govern our lives. So maybe I'd get lucky and find Girolama Spera's address which I currently didn't have. It's worth a try.

When I search for people named Girolama Spera, the only entries that show-up are the references to her namesake's involvement in the *Aqua Tofana* murders. I try just Spera and the artist's website does come up. It's one of those stock sites you can buy already configured so all you have to do is plug-in your text and images. The website has no personal information or contact numbers other than Greyson's email and phone number. It identifies him as her agent. The rest of the site is dominated by images of her paintings and a few watercolours.

When I get to Greyson's building, I go directly to the rental office and flash my pretty new Detective Chief Inspector's badge. I'm given the key and head for the top floor. Greyson had good taste. The place is filled with Rennie Mackintosh furniture and the walls are covered in Spera's colourful oils. The only disquieting aspect of the place is that it's a mess. The furniture has been knocked over and the drawers emptied with the contents dumped on the floor. Most of the paintings have been taken off the walls and ripped out of their frames. Pieces of picture frame moulding litter the Chinese carpet. I never quite understood why criminals can't be neat when they ransack somebody's home. It's just a matter of courtesy, after all, you break-in and steal everything of value, I figure the least you can do is not make a mess of the place.

I look around, rummaging through the debris but find nothing of interest other than a diary used to schedule appointments. I leaf through the pages.

The one regular entry that peaks my interest simply reads 'Meet Tiger.' I check to see if there's a directory in the back of the diary, there is. I skim through the names looking for anything that relates to Tiger but find nothing... nothing except the name Yang Hu, and an address in Chinatown. Yang is a common Chinese name, but really, what are the chances of this being a coincidence? It's time for some Chinese takeaway.

When I get to Yang's flat I knock on the door. She opens the door as far as the chain lock allows. "Can I help you?" Her face has splashes of Indian Red across her forehead.

"May I come in?" I flash my police badge. She hesitates, but unlatches the chain and moves aside.

"What is this about?"

The flat is a combination of home and studio. It's filled with the familiar tools of the artist's trade. Her paintings, drawings, and watercolours are everywhere. I am intrigued. I walk past her taking note of her work. I pick up one of her watercolours; it is better than I originally thought.

"You're Yang Hu, aka, Tiger?"

"Yes."

"You use the name Girolama Spera as a professional name for your paintings."

"Yes."

"Interesting name."

"It's historical."

"I am aware."

I turn to look at her. Her hands are on her hips. She's attractive in a manner I would not call pretty. Interesting is a better description. She's sexy without trying. Her features are all wrong, but somehow they work together. I take her all in. "Very nice." Her eyes narrow. "The work I mean."

"You'll have to speak to my agent if you want to buy something."

"Mr. Greyson? He's dead, as I'm sure you already know." I continue to move around the flat looking for something that doesn't belong, something that will give her away. She continues to stand with her hands on her hips.

"Do you have a search warrant?" I ignore the question. I brush back my jacket so she can see the Beretta, just in case she needs some encouragement to cooperate. She knows London cops don't normally carry firearms. She gets the message and decides to play along.

"Is this about D.D.? He was killed in a traffic accident, a hit and run."

"I guess the poison didn't work fast enough."

She remains calm, visibly relaxes. She notices my reaction. She smiles, "Who are you?" I don't answer. She turns and heads for a desk in the corner of the room. I remove the Beretta from the shoulder holster. She sees my reflection in the glass of a framed watercolour hanging on the wall. "If you were going to shoot me, you'd have done it already."

"Just being cautious."

"May I open the desk drawer to get my passport?"

"No." She stops, not taking any chances.

"Get on the floor, face down with your hands on your head." She does what she's told. "Spread your legs."

"We can go in the bedroom if you like?"

I nudge her legs apart with my foot. I pat her down. Something is strapped to the inside of her leg. I place my knee in the small of her back so she can't move. She groans just a little from the pressure. I remove the AKC 6" Switchblade from the sheath strapped to her leg and put it in my pocket. "If you don't want a hole in your some-what, attractive head, don't fucking move!" I re-move my leg from her back and move to the desk. I open the drawer. She wasn't exactly lying. Her passport is sitting beside a Glock G26. I shove the gun in my jacket pocket. I pick up her passport, and a ticket to *The Innovation Britain Expo* falls out. Is this the breadcrumb Harriet was talking about? I stick both in the inside pocket of my sport coat.

"I have diplomatic immunity, so I suggest..."

"Shut up!"

"Who are you?"

"Someone who doesn't give a shit about diplomatic immunity."

I hear a car drive up and stop outside the building. I glance out the window. It's the red SUV.

"Who's in the Land Rover?"

"What are you talking about?"

"What's your relationship with Yang Guozhi?"

"He's my *Shushu*... Uncle."

"Jesus... that son-of-a-bitch uses his own niece?"

"I don't work for him."

"So, who do you work for?"

"I want a lawyer."

I laugh. "Sure sweetheart, I'll get right on that." I use Hu's phone to call 999, London's version of 911. "Please come quick, there's a red Land Rover that's been following me all day. It's parked out in front of my flat." I give the operator the address and hang up. I dial Roger and fill him in on what I've done.

"Bring her to Quandary. We'll interrogate her there." I hang up. I hear another vehicle pull up in front of the building. It's the police. They approach the Land Rover.

I find a roll of Duck tape hanging on the corner of an easel. "Rollover." I pat her down again, making sure I didn't miss any more hidden weapons.

"Enjoying yourself."

"In a matter of speaking." I duck tape her hands behind her back. "Are you going to behave or do I tape your mouth shut?"

She shrugs, "I'll behave. You can't do shit to me. I have diplomatic cover and friends in high places."

"I know your Uncle, I wouldn't count on that son-of-a-bitch to help you."

"Maybe… but I have lots of relatives."

"Come on, get up. We're going for a ride." We make our way down the stairs and out of the building. The cops are still hassling the two men from the SUV. I can't see their faces but from the gesturing, they are not happy.

I notice a black Mercedes pull up behind the cop car. A tall, middle-aged man in a pinstripe suit approaches the police. He flashes some kind of identification. The cops practically snap to attention. It's time to get the hell out of there.

I shove Yang into the passenger seat, get in, and drive a couple of blocks down the street. I turn into a darkened alley filled with trash cans from the numerous Chinese restaurants that dominate the block, most of whom seem to cater to Chinese patrons. I often wonder if Chinese people ever eat at home, based on the number of Cantonese, Sichuan, and Shandong restaurants in the area, all of whom seem to be full, all the time. I get out of the car, open the boot, and go around to the passenger side door. The smell in the alley is overwhelming. "Get out."

'You got to be fucking kidding? What? Did you see this in a movie or something?"

"In fact, yes… in a movie or something." I pull her out of the car and dump her in the boot. She looks up at me with a bemused look on her face.

"Ever see *Jackie Brown*? Just think of me as Sam Jackson and you as Chris Tucker." She starts to say something but I slam the trunk lid closed before she can get it out.

Three Blind Mice

Three blind mice. Three blind mice.
See how they run. See how they run.
They all ran after the farmer's wife,
Who cuts off their tails with a carving knife,
Did you ever see such a sight in your life,
As three blind mice?

I arrive at Quandary Research about fifteen minutes too late. The fire department, police, and ambulances are already there. The building that housed Roger's little covert enterprise is consumed in flames. Several body bags are being loaded into two coroner vans. I get out of the car and approach a policeman keeping the gathered crowd behind the yellow tape. I flash my badge.

"Could you tell me what happened here?"

"Yes, Sir. It seems there was an explosion. The LFB doesn't believe it was a faulty gas-line. It's more than a little suspicious. The place was mostly empty. Only one tenant, a research firm with a shitload of computers and electronic gear. Whatever they were researching, somebody didn't want it found."

"I see some people were killed."

"Yes, Sir, three, the rest of the staff had gone home."

"Any survivors?" The cop points to a paramedic attending to someone who looks familiar. It's Roger. He's sitting on the end of an ambulance in a rather bad state, Roger, not the ambulance. His head is bandaged. There are bloodstains on his face, and his clothes are torn and bloody. I approach. "Jesus, Roger, what the hell happened?"

"It seems we're getting too bloody close. Someone wants to shut us down... permanently."

"It's us now, is it?"

"You're it, dear boy. You're all I got. Everyone else that's left is tech. You're the only field man I got still working on this thing." I ignore the irony of my sudden inclusive status. He attempts to get up but falters. "Can you take me home, Harry? I don't have time for the hospital."

"Don't be stupid, you've probably got a concussion or worse."

"I wasn't even in the building. I just arrived to wait for you and the woman when the explosion tore the place apart. I got hit by some flying de-

bris. I'll be fine, but I need to get out of here before the cops or the LFB start asking questions."

"All right, but take it easy."

We walk back to my car. The short walk is ex-
hausting for him. He leans against the back door
of the car to rest. "Where's the woman?"

I go to the boot and open it. Roger looks in, he
starts to laugh but the exertion hurts too much.
Hu starts to say something but I slam the lid shut.
We both lean on the boot saying nothing. A black
limousine pulls up behind us. It has Chinese
diplomatic plates. We wait.

The driver gets out of the car and opens the back
door. An older, well-dressed Chinese man gets
out. He says a few words to the driver who wan-
ders off towards the police cordon. He approaches us. It's Yang Guozhi, Head of the Enterprise
Division of the Ministry of State Security. "Roger,
old friend, are you okay?"

"I'll survive."

"And you, Harry… how have you been?"

"Did you do this, Yang, cause if you did…" Roger takes my arm, partially to shut me up, and partially to steady himself.

Yang tries to make peace. "The three of us have had our differences, but in this matter, we are all on the same side."

I don't respond, it's better to let things play out and see what side each of us eventually lands on.

"So, Harry, you've been a very busy boy. Where's my niece?"

"You have a niece?"

Roger looks at me, "Show him." I open the lid of the boot. The three of us look down at Yang Hu curled up in the trunk with her hands taped behind her back. She looks up at her Uncle, "*Nǐ hǎo shūshu.*" I slam the boot lid shut.

The ever-present red Land Rover followed by a black Mercedes pulls up beside us blocking the street. A tall, middle-aged man in a pinstripe suit gets out of the back of the Mercedes. "Well, well, if it isn't the three blind mice."

Yang's driver, who was watching the fire, notices the Mercedes' arrival. He starts walking back, but when he gets to the German luxury sedan, he bends over to retie his shoelaces, which is curious. He's wearing loafers. The driver sticks his hand in his pocket and takes out a small box. He places it on the inside of the Mercedes' fender. He uses the bumper to help himself up. The entire charade only takes a few seconds. No one else seems to notice, no one except Yang and me.

Both Roger and Yang recognize who he is. Yang speaks first, "Charlie, a pleasure as always. Have you met our friend, Harry?"

I stick out my hand. He shakes it but doesn't let go. "Aah, Roger's pet rat." I don't answer. "You know, I can't do anything about Yang and probably not Roger and his unauthorized clan of high tech hyenas, but you, on the other hand, are left hung out to dry."

Roger interrupts, "Let it go, Charlie, he's my man, that's the end of it."

"Does someone want to tell me who this is?"

Roger steadies himself by grasping my arm, "This is Elite Officer Charles T. Thompson... MI5."

The politics of the internal and external Intelligence Services is byzantine at best. Conflicts and cooperation go hand-in-hand in the bureaucratic empire-building within and between the rival agencies. The rules only apply if you get caught, and as the Americans have shown, if you are high enough on the food chain, getting caught is merely a nuisance. What the elected politicians don't know, or at least, pretend not to know, won't stain their knickers. And so, our *frienemies* at MI5 are well aware of Quandary but have seemingly decided to turn a blind eye.

Quandary had the advantage of doing things the official agency apparatuses weren't supposed to do, but nevertheless wanted done. MI5 didn't squawk because Roger's Vauxhall Cross masters could not take credit for Quandary's wins but stood vulnerable to take the fall for their losses. The real source of conflict between Roger and Charlie Thompson was sharing information.

So, Thompson was resigned to the existence of Roger's side project. How Yang fits in is another impenetrable matter.

Thompson looks at Roger, "You know we had bugs in the niece's flat. Between you, me, and Uncle Yang, there is enough electronic gear in that place to bring in BMN (Beijing Media Network).

Thompson looks at me, "You have the girl?"

"I believe, woman, is the more politically correct term when referring to a female adult."

"Where is she?" I ignore him.

He looks at Roger, "This will not end well for you, Ames if you don't turn her over." Roger follows my lead and says nothing.

Thompson turns to Yang, "It's a bear market for you, Yang, your brother's stock is rising and yours is being shorted. Beijing is more interested in getting their hands on new tech than they are on selling more shit to Tesco. They will not be happy with you getting in their way."

Yang smiles. "It's very curious why MI5 would not want my assistance in this matter. Perhaps, it's you, Charlie, that wants things to go my brother's way, you and not MI5, you and not my friends in Beijing."

Thompson shrugs, turns, and waves to his min-ions that they're leaving. He gets in the back of the Mercedes and the two cars drive off.

Yang nudges me. I look down. He's handing me a prepaid mobile phone. "A present, to show good faith. Use it to call me anytime, Harry, anytime. I will make myself available. I do hope we can become good friends." He waves to his driver and they leave the area.

Roger and I both look down at the phone. It's tracking Charlie Thompson's Mercedes. Roger smiles. "Well done, old chap, well done."

"Now what?"

"We need to debrief the niece. Let's take her to your place."

"I got a better idea."

I use my mobile phone to call my partner in the restaurant-jazz club that I partly own. "Sidney, it's me. Meet me in The Smoke Shop."

The Smoke Shop

The Smoke Shop is the restaurant and jazz club that I rescued from bankruptcy. My partner, Sidney Katz, bought the old ironworks buildings and proceeded to blow his brains out financially. The cost of turning the ground-floor of Building One into an Art Deco style restaurant, bar, and entertainment complex with loft-style flats on the second and third floors was substantial. The gallery is located beside the restaurant in Building Two.

Sidney needed my help in making his dream come true and I needed a base of operation in London. We may have started as business partners but over the last few months, we have become good friends. Sidney understands that I do something beyond investing in property and owning art galleries. I'm sure he thinks whatever I do is illegal, or at least shady, and as you know, his assessment is not exactly incorrect. He probably thinks I'm some kind of Jay Gatsby type character which suits me fine; since Sidney sees himself as a Baldy Jack Rose style club owner. So when I ask to use the restaurant basement, no questions asked, he's eager to oblige. Hu's colleagues might come looking for her in the gallery but they'd have no interest in The Smoke Shop.

We park in the back of the restaurant. It's dark, so we're not concerned with being seen removing Hu from the boot of the car. We take her down to The Smoke Shop basement that's filled with a variety of Art Deco chairs, tables, restaurant paraphernalia, and a rather extensive wine cellar, something that might come in handy if Hu's interrogation becomes a lengthy process.

We place Hu in a wooden chair with her hands duct-taped behind her back and her ankles duct-taped to the legs of the chair. Roger takes a matching seat and places it in front of her. I sit off to the side in a more comfortable dark brown Art Deco Club chair. Roger stares at Hu without saying a word. He rubs his neck. He's still in pain from the explosion. "You killed Jimmy Cotton." She doesn't answer.

"I've never heard of Jimmy Cotton. Who's he."

Roger doesn't remove his eyes from Hu. "Jimmy was one of my people. He was a plant in the development department of Britco Telcom. We know everything about what you were doing."

She smirks, "Not everything."

"Who blew up my building?" She doesn't answer.

"Who's your handler?" She merely stares back.

"Who are your contacts?" Still no answer.

Finally, she speaks, "You know, I'm not going to answer. I have diplomatic immunity."

"You're assuming I care."

"You should care. My father is Yang Bo, Minister of Science and Technology. If you arrest me or harm me in any way, there will be consequences."

I decide to put in my two cents, "You know, Greyson kept copious journals on your activity. Is that why you poisoned him?

She sneers, "I believe he was killed in a traffic accident, not by poison."

Roger stands. He moves closer, almost touching her. "You shouldn't have used an embassy vehicle with embassy plates." She looks surprised that we know this information. She shrugs as best she can with her hands duct-taped behind her back.

"Last chance, Hu." She doesn't answer.

Roger takes his phone out of his pocket and dials, "Carlos, It's Roger Ames. I need your expert assistance in a matter of extreme discretion."

You can hear what sounds like a thick Portuguese accent on the other end of the line. Roger's friend is probably Brazilian, and if it's who I think it is, it's not good news for Hu. "That's right Carlos, bring your black bag." Roger puts his phone back in his pocket. He turns to me. "You better leave. There's no need for you to see this."

"Roger, are you sure you want to do this?"

"She killed D. D. Greyson, Jimmy Cotton, and three more of my people, she spied on our country and stole top-secret technology. You're fucking right I want to do this."

I've never seen Roger lose his cool. It's refreshing. The man does have a heart. I get into my car without any idea of where I'm going. I still have Hu's passport, switchblade, and Glock in my jacket. I place her Glock in the glovebox. I'm still carrying the Beretta so I don't need the Glock. I take Hu's passport out of my jacket pocket; perhaps it will point me in the right direction. The ticket to the *Innovation Britain Expo* falls out.

I remember what Harriet said, "We might run into one another at the Expo." I look at the date. The trade show and conference started today. I check my watch, the evening session is still open. I decide to check the mobile phone with the tracker that Guozhi gave me. The address on the phone is the same as the convention centre. All the breadcrumbs lead to the same place.

Show and Tell

All trade shows and conferences are the same. It doesn't matter what the merchants are hawking; the products, the people, and the environment are always interchangeable. The overly enthusiastic young man wearing the off-the-rack suit and wireless microphone headset pitching the wondrous things you can do with the latest vegetable dicer might as well be the guy pitching foreign Generals and government officials on the latest high tech hardware. If you've been to one trade show convention, you've been to them all.

I purchase a VIP ticket that's worth one hundred pounds but I get a ten percent discount when I present my phoney police credentials. It's expensive, but it does give me free access to the trade show, conference area, and special meeting rooms where corporate and government buyers eat, drink, and negotiate contracts.

As you enter the show floor, you're handed a plastic bag filled with crap from merchants who pay extra for the privilege of loading you down with cheap pens, flash drives, and other useless gadgets with their company logos printed on them in bold colours. One startup that specializes in anti-virus protection software thought it clever to provide convention visitors with condoms emblazoned with the image of an elephant in gaudy pink. I suppose the idea was to think of them when you're getting screwed. I deposited the whole lot in the first waste bin I came across.

Like all trade shows, there are multiple rows of booths; some are big, flashy, and expensive, while others are merely tables draped in blue cloth with the suppliers' wares neatly displayed.

I make my way up and down a few aisles when I spot a familiar figure. About ten yards in front of me is a woman in tight black jeans and a grey hoodie with the Toronto Blue Jays logo on the back. Even though I can't see her face, I sense it's Harriet; the hoodie is her way of saying follow my lead. She stops at a German audio manufacturer displaying a variety of eavesdropping gear aimed at police departments.

An attractive saleswoman in an overtly sexy outfit showing far too much skin approaches Harriet reciting her well-memorized pitch for a wireless directional microphone-recorder that's disguised as a biro pen. She has repeated the same bollocks several hundred times during the day.

The woman flips the hoodie down and turns towards me, it's not Harriet. She smiles. The saleswoman notices. She excuses herself and approaches me, repeating the same pitch word-for-word, but with far more body English. She leans over the table while presenting the small device, allowing me a rather breathtaking view of her well-endowed merchandise.

"How much?"

"It's one-hundred-and-fifty pounds, but if you represent a police department I can offer a deep discount with an official purchase order."

"I show her my DCI Caul badge."

"I can knock-off fifteen percent."

"Okay, I'll take this one."

"Oh, this one is not for sale, but I can accept a purchase order and have the office send one out to you tomorrow."

The hoodie woman coughs to draw attention. "Excuse me, I'd like to know more about that microphone." She points to the most expensive unit displayed on the back wall of the booth.

The saleswoman waves, "I'll be there as soon as I finish with this gentleman."

"Go ahead. I need to check with my boss to get a purchase order." I thank the woman for her expert assistance. She insists that I take her card and call her... any time. She rejoins the hoodie lady who starts asking a series of highly technical questions in what seems like an effort to flummox the saleswoman. The tired saleswoman goes to the back of the booth to retrieve the microphone the hoodie lady demands to see. I slip the unit on the table into my pocket. I take one-hundred-and-fifty pounds out of my billfold and slip it under the now empty box. I wave goodbye to the attractive saleswoman and head down the aisle towards the snack-bar area.

The hoodie woman thanks the frustrated saleswoman and follows me around the next group of booths. She passes me and heads for the snack-bar area where I see Harriet waiting for me at a table. I order two coffees and join her. I place one of the coffees in front of her knowing she won't drink it. Apparitions don't drink.

Harriet turns to me with an odd look on her face. "You'd make a good thief."

"I paid for it. It cost me one-hundred-and-fifty-quid. It might come in handy. "

"Maybe… Charlie Thompson is here."

"I know."

"He's meeting Yang Bo."

"Why?"

"Roger had the Brazilian drug Hu, and inject her with a tracker so he could keep an eye on her without her knowing. She had no reason to talk; she has diplomatic immunity. Roger knew he had to release her or turn her over to Charlie Thompson, so he drove her home and waited to see what she did next. Roger and Guozhi think Thompson is Bo's inside-man. "

"Are they sure?"

"Well, she went directly to Thompson instead of her father or the embassy. She must desperately want to salvage something out of the operation, but Charlie knows she's blown and wants her out of his hair before he's found out."

"So how's Charlie going to explain turning her over to the Chinese?"

"He doesn't have to. He doesn't know she's got a tracker embedded in her neck. He thinks Roger and you will assume she went to her father as soon as she was released?"

"She burned Charlie Thompson. Even I know that's a pretty amateurish move."

"She's desperate. Being Yang Bo's kid only works in your favour if you don't fuck-up, and she's fucked-up."

"We need to find out where they're making the exchange so we can get hard evidence on Thompson. I can use the pen-mic if I can get close enough. All I have to do is aim it in their direction. I'll use my phone to get video."

"Just watch out for Bo's bodyguards. I'll check out the meeting rooms. You check out the kitchens. There's a kosher kitchen that's not being used for this event. Maybe they'll do the exchange there."

"Be careful, my love, you're no good to me or Mercury with a hole in your head." She kisses me on the cheek and disappears into a crowd.

Kitchen Exchange

I make my way to the kitchens. There are two kitchens behind the trade show floor area. One is a noisy beehive of activity with people scurrying around prepping the dinner that's being held after the trade show closes for the evening. The other kitchen is silent but the light is on. I carefully enter, doing my best not to make a noise. I hear voices. I position myself behind a shelf containing paper towels, napkins, and canned food. I can't make out what's being said and the paper products hide my view.

I place the pen-mic on a shelf between two large rolls of paper towels. I lean my mobile up against a package of coloured napkins that helps disguise the presence of my phone. I move down the aisle trying to find an opening so I can see what's happening.

I feel a large hand on my shoulder. Whoever it is, swings me around. All I see is a fist coming at my head. I duck, avoiding a direct hit but the blow manages to land on my ear. We struggle with each of us landing punches; then things go dark.

I awake with some kind of burlap bag over my head, probably a potato sack evidenced by the smell. The loose weave of the fabric allows me to barely make out the shapes of at least four people. They stand over me arguing in Chinese.

There are two distinct older male Chinese voices and one younger female voice, the female is most assuredly Yang Hu. One of the older Chinese men sounds a lot like Yang Guozhi and the other must be his brother Bo. The fourth person is Charlie Thompson, I recognize his voice when he whispers, "Kill the motherfucker! He has no official status. Neither agency will give a shit."

I hear Guozhi object, "*Méiyǒu!*"

There is some further muttering in Chinese and English. I remain calm pretending to be unconscious. My arms are tied behind my back wrapped around one of the shelves. My head hurts and I can taste blood dripping down into my mouth from my nose. Everything from there on is a muddle. There is more arguing that sounds like a discussion about whether or not to put a bullet in my head. They settle for several kicks to my midsection and a final blow to my head that does render me unconscious again.

I don't know how long I was out. I'm not in good shape, every bone in my body hurts. I'm still tied to the shelf but the job was slapdash. Despite my hands being tied behind my back, I do have enough freedom of movement to reach my pocket where I put Hu's switchblade. I manage to get at the knife, but releasing the blade and manipulating it into a position to cut the nylon rope they used to tie me up takes some time. I finally cut myself free. The lights in the kitchen are off, so I can't see a goddamn thing. I feel my way to the door and turn them on.

I find my way back to where I was attacked. My Beretta is on the floor about ten feet away from where I was tied up. I go to where I hid the microphone. Thank goodness, it's still where I left it, but who knows if it captured anything useable.

My phone faired even worse. It got knocked off the shelf onto the floor, where it recorded some great video of the ceiling, however, it did manage to pick up some of the audio. I'll check it once I get home and my head recovers a bit from the beating. They took the burner with the Charlie Thompson tracker on it. I feel sick to my stomach. I'm able to make my way to the washrooms despite the fact the trade show is dark and everything seems to be closed for the night.

I wash my face and clean off the blood as best I can. I manage to avoid throwing up. Finally, I make my way out into the parking lot, find my car, and head home.

On arriving home, I notice a limousine parked in front of the gallery. I park in my usual spot behind the building and make my way to the front. The back window of the limo rolls down. It's Guozhi. "Are you all right, my friend?"

"You were there?"

"Yes, I crashed their little party. Come sit." I move to the other side of the limo and get in. Guozhi hands me a brandy from the bar in front of him. "Here, you could use this. You don't look well."

I'm not much of a drinker but I figure now is as good a time as any to make an exception. I take a sip of the brandy. "It was you that stopped them from putting a bullet in my head?"

"Yes."

"Thanks."

"I like you, Harry, you're a very interesting fellow. And quite useful on occasion."

"Good to know."

"They looked for your phone, but it wasn't in your pockets. Did you capture the exchange?"

"Nah, it fell on the floor. All I got was the ceiling of the kitchen." I don't mention the pen-mic. He doesn't have to know everything.

"Too bad. Evidence of Charlie Thompson turning my niece over to my brother would put an end to him and this whole unfortunate mess."

"MI5 would have had to turn her over eventually, so Thompson could claim he was just trying to avoid an international incident."

"True, but I'm sure they'd want to interrogate her first to find out who else is involved. That's why my brother and Thompson wanted to eliminate you. You know too much."

"Why are you doing this. It could be seen as treason by Beijing. You could end up on the other end of a firing squad."

"I told you when we met in Washington, China's prosperity relies on trade. We need to eliminate sanctions and eventually tariffs. Corporate espionage is short-sighted. All it does is piss-off your customers and create friction. Besides, anything we steal, we can develop ourselves."

"You mean, buy it, reverse engineer it, and ignore any patents."

Guozhi ignores my comment but smiles. "That's why I like you, Harry, we understand each other."

"I need to get some aspirin, your goons did a real job on me."

"It was Thompson. He wants you dead and he hasn't given up on the idea. You know too much and are far too dangerous to let continue." He hands me a new tracker-phone. "They found the first device but I had my driver install another."

"Thanks."

"Let Roger know the score, he should be able to provide some protection. And Harry…" He pauses not sure whether to tell me what he's thinking, "Charlie Thompson isn't the only one on my brother's payroll. He's got someone in MI6 as well, someone very close and very dangerous."

"Do you know who?"

"No."

"You're playing a dangerous game, Yang. It could very easily backfire. Not everyone in Beijing is as enlightened as you. Be careful."

The Seven Dwarfs

I enter my flat with nothing more on my mind other than finding my bed and collapsing. Once inside I notice all the lights are on and someone seems to be having a party. I draw my Beretta and make my way around a large bookshelf that hides my view. "Come in, Harry, we've been waiting for you." It's Roger and six other people I've never seen before. Roger gives me a closer look. "You are a sight, dear boy. Sit. I'll fix you a drink."

"No thanks, Guozhi already plied me with brandy. Another will put me right to sleep.

Roger ignores my objection. He gets me a brandy from the bar that's generally reserved for invited guests. One of Roger's cohorts asks if he can sample the bar. I have no objection. My six new acquaintances adjourn to the free liquor supply like a horde of Manchurian horseman.

"You saw Guozhi?"

"Twice." I recount the events of the evening as quickly and quietly as possible while his friends decide on how much of my booze they can politely consume.

"So the Circus has a new mole. That's what Guozhi told you?"

"Yes. Close and dangerous."

"I hope you still don't find me suspect?"

"No, Roger, I've come to realize your intentions are generally on the right side of things, even if they're not always pure."

"Dear boy, neither of us could pass a purity test. You'll have to admit, your's could do with a thorough washing."

I smile. What can I say? He's right. "Let's keep the news of a second spider to ourselves for now."

"We need to tell them. They can't do their jobs if we don't. I trust these people, but I understand your concern, temptation lurks in the most unexpected places."

Roger's friends rejoin us from the bar, each with their selected liquid refreshment. Roger immediately takes charge. They all stop talking and pay attention. "We are what's left of Quandary Research. I know none of you have met, Harry, but you are aware of his work on the Yang Hu business." They all nod.

"So now I'm part of the group?"

"You were always part of the group, dear boy, even in Toronto and Washington. You just didn't know it."

"Does Vauxhall Cross know about it or is this your little secret?" I can almost feel the others in the room stiffen. "I'd like to know where I stand."

"For all it's worth, you always had official status, Harry. It's all in a file, in a box, locked in a drawer marked Top Secret, along with the files for everyone else in this room. That said, any of us screw the pooch as our American friends are fond of saying, and we're on our own."

One of my guests, the roly-poly one, decides to join the conversation, "Welcome to the club, mate. Sweet flat."

"Introductions seem in order. This is Graham…" A tall thin reed of a man in his late twenties, nods in my direction.

"Milo…" My new roly-poly mate is a thirty-five-year-old, overweight, ball of haphazardly assembled body parts. He rises from the couch to shake my hand.

"Edward…" Another interchangeable millennial nods in my direction.

"Kevin…" A fifty-something man in a well-tailored Savile Row suit stands to shake my hand.

"Darlene…" A woman who could pass for your standard soccer mom, smiles and waves.

"And Melinda…" A very attractive woman in a bespoke chalk-stripe pantsuit acknowledges me with a dismissive wave of my liquor.

Roger: "The first order of business is to find a new base of operations and new equipment. Everything that wasn't destroyed in the explosion was collected by Graham and stored in a locker. I doubt anything can be retrieved…"

Milo: "I can give it a try boss, maybe something can be salvaged."

Darlene: "What about backup."

Milo: "In a safe place. We find a new location and equipment and we can be up and running in a day, fully operational in two."

Roger: "Melinda, can you find us a place?"

Before she can answer, I speak up. "Perhaps I can help with that. Do you have a budget?"

Darlene: "We've got money in the kitty, but we also need to spend some on gear. and that stuff is expensive. Our Vauxhall masters are as tight as a virgin's twat." Everyone smiles.

"The flat over The Smoke Shop, next store, is vacant. I can arrange it with my partner for us to rent it. It's about two thousand square feet."

Roger: "That's perfect. Melinda's a lawyer, she can work out the details with you or your partner. Milo and Graham will look after acquiring the new gear. Kevin, you let the boys at headquarters know what we're doing. Darlene, you help Milo and Graham."

Melinda: "And what's Harry's brief, other than real estate?"

Roger: "Harry works with me. He's our man on the ground. You give him whatever he wants."

Darlene: "No offence, Harry, but shouldn't we check with you first?"

Roger: "You give Harry whatever the fuck he wants. If he opens his mouth, the words that come out are mine."

Everyone in the room, including me is a bit taken back by Roger's vociferous backing of my status as the obvious second-in-command.

Roger: "The next order of business is phones. No personal mobiles. Once we leave this room, nobody refers to another member of the group on a phone by their real name. Milo has given each of us a cryptonym. Remember who's who."

Milo urges his substantial bulk off my couch and starts handing out phones from a plastic bag he had resting at his feet. He seems to be the Jack Black character in our very off-Broadway play. "Okay fellow deviants, from now on we are collectively the Seven Dwarfs: I'm Flick, Graham's Blick, Edward's Glick, Kevin's Plick, Darlene's Whick, Melinda is Snick, and Harry is Quee. Roger is the Huntsman."

Darlene: "What happened to Dopey, Doc, and whatever the others are called?"

Graham: "Bashful, Happy, Grumpy…"

Edward: Sleepy and Sneezy."

Melinda: "Really? It's like working with a group of oversized children."

Roger: "Enough. Just remember everybody's co-dename and phone number. It's all entered in each of your phones."

Melinda: "Do we have a target?"

Roger looks at me and then the group. "Yang Hu is still out there, but she's untouchable. She has diplomatic immunity because of her father."

Kevin: "Since when has that stopped us. She's never had any close security. I could arrange for an accident to happen. It would serve her right."

Roger: "She's burned, so I doubt they'll trust her with anything hands-on, but she is Yang Bo's kid, so you never know. Keep an eye on her, she might lead us to a new target."

Milo: "There's a new target?"

Roger: "Close and dangerous."

I give Roger a look. The others notice. "Sorry, Harry, I think the others need to know."

Melinda: "Who's the target?"

Roger: "Yet to be identified."

Milo: "Our new quarry is codenamed, Grim, if it's male and, Grimhilde, if it's female."

Roger: "Okay, everyone has their instructions. Melinda, you work out the rental agreement with Harry, under one of our shell companies. And Harry, you arrange for us to get into the flat tomorrow. Hopefully, that won't be a problem. We need to move fast."

"I'll call my partner and let him know I've rented the place. He'll be happy it's off-the-market and generating some cash."

Everyone gets up and heads for the door. Roger lingers behind. Once they all leave, Roger asks what I think of the group?

"Hard to tell, to be honest. I can't say I got a good handle on all of them. They seem okay, I guess, but Melinda and Kevin seem to be outliers. They're more mature, better dressed, and more sophisticated than the others."

"Kevin adds needed experience to the group. He's been around awhile, close to retirement, and he has deep political and interagency contacts. At his stage of the game, he has nothing to prove."

"And Melinda, what's her story?"

"She's a lawyer. She came over from Five. She's the price Six had to pay to get Five to let us operate. If everything goes from pudding to poop, we can claim she makes us a Five operation. She's here to make sure we don't push the envelope too far. She's kind of our taskmasters' Scully to your Mulder."

"I thought pushing the envelope was exactly what we're here to do."

"Yes, push the envelope as long as we don't get caught. She's here to protect the Ring Masters, not the Clowns. Perhaps that's what you sensed. I've always said you have good instincts."

"If she's from Five, how do we know she's not feeding Charlie Thompson with intel on everything we're doing? She could be the spider."

"I'll have Milo monitor the situation."

"One more thing, Roger. Harriet, is she one of us? It's about time I knew the whole truth."

Roger doesn't answer immediately. "You like movies, don't you, Harry?"

"What does that have to do with it?"

"Jack Nicholson, *A Few Good Men,* excellent movie. It's not your Film Noir kind of thing, I know, but still, some great dialogue."

Static

The next morning I wake, still feeling the effects of the night before. I shower, shave, and start to make breakfast. After all the excitement of yesterday, the place seems oppressively quiet. I turn on the television to see if there's any news of note; there isn't. I turn down the sound but keep the visual just in case something interesting appears on the screen. I turn on the radio to fill the dead air. I search for, and find, the jazz station; they're playing *Poinciana* by Ahmad Jamal, but it keeps cutting-out and there's a lot of static.

That's very strange. There is no reason why my over-priced stereo system is suddenly having issues. I rarely have guests, in fact, I can't recall the last time anyone has been in my flat, other than me or Billy. Last night's impromptu get-together meant strangers had free rein of my place. I am by nature a suspicious person. Having Roger and my six new mates wandering around my flat, suddenly made me very nervous. I have no idea what they were doing before I arrived. I do know everyone gathered around the bar. I decide to check it out. I bend down and look under the rosewood bar top... and there it is, a bug.

The spider is not just closer than I suspected; it appears that he or she is also more aggressively audacious. The bug under the bar seems to be too obvious, a decoy, perhaps, for one or more well-hidden devices, maybe even video. It's a standard tradecraft maneuver. Let the mark feel safe by providing some low hanging fruit, while the real juicy stuff is high up out of reach. I leave the bug where I found it. Roger and I will have to have a talk. I call him on my new phone. It beeps, prompting me to leave a message. "It's me, we need to talk, my favourite café, twelve o'clock."

I finish breakfast and go downstairs to check in with Billy. I admit to being rather slack in my gallery ownership duties, but Billy has turned out to be more than competent and my services don't add anything to the mix. Mercury trained him well. I enter the gallery and Billy waves me over, "Morning, Boss." He looks me over with more than a little concern, "Jesus, Harry, I hope the other guy faired even worse."

"Sorry to say, I didn't land a blow. I got suckered."

"You should go back to bed."

"Can't. Things to do."

"I'll bet. More sinister plots to uncover and evil-doers to foil?"

"Don't let your imagination get the best of you, Billy-boy."

"What do you want me to do with the package?"

"Package?"

"It came this morning." Billy points to a box on his desk."

I check it out. There isn't a return address. I'm not up for something blowing up in my face and Billy is just an innocent bystander. "Perhaps you shouldn't stand so close." Billy stands back a few paces for all the good that will do if it's a bomb. I open the box.

No explosion. Billy hovers over my shoulder, "What are they?" There are six silver *mezuzot* and a phone.

"They're *mezuzot*. Inside the silver-case is a special hand-written prayer that protects you from evil. You attach them to the doorpost of your home. The Orthodox put one on the entrance to each room." Billy picks one up to inspect it. I turn on the phone. An image pops up on the screen, it's Billy staring down at the *mezuzah*.

I show him. "They're cameras."

There's a note in the box. I pick it up. "*Protect yourself, Harry, evil lurks in every doorway. Be careful my love. - H*" I stick the note in my pocket.

"Who's it from?"

"A friend."

"What are you going to do with them?"

"You're going to install them in my flat." Even though my place is an open plan loft, the living spaces are demarcated by glass brick dividers that provide for separation and privacy. "Put one on the outside of the front door and spread the rest around for maximum coverage."

"You're expecting trouble?"

I ignore Billy's question. "I have a meeting, I have to go. Make sure they're installed today." I leave and head for my meeting with Roger.

By the time I get to George's Café, Roger is already there having a cup of tea. I sit down and George, the owner, brings my usual coffee.

"I found a bug."

"*Shite!* They must have heard everything we said last night."

"For sure, but whoever it was, didn't need a bug."

"What do you mean?"

"I found it under the bar where everyone gathered for drinks. One of them must have placed it there while cocktails were being served."

"Did you remove it?"

"No. Now I know it's there, maybe we can use it to our advantage."

"There may be more. It might just be a decoy."

"My thoughts exactly. We need to do a sweep."

"What did you think of Milo?"

"Milo? Seems okay. He's the joker of the group, but that might be his way of hiding in plain sight. Never trust a clown."

"True. It could be any of them. I'll get a hold of a gadget and meet you back at your flat. We'll do the job together. Even unscrew the electrical plates and check the lights for cameras."

"Harriet sent me some cameras connected to a phone app. Billy is installing them now. They're hidden in *mezuzot*, we'll leave those in place."

"Harriet sent them? Are you sure it was Harriet?"

"Yes. Harriet, my so-called imaginary friend."

"I hope the pressure isn't starting to get to you. This is too important to screw up."

The Spider's Web

Spider, Spider On The Wall
If You Get Caught
You'll Take The Fall

Melinda Byrne leaves her flat headed for her dark red Jaguar XF parked out in front of her luxury condo. She notices her ex-gaffer, Charlie Thompson, leaning against the door of her car. He gives her a perfunctory nod while grasping her hand as if he's handing her something. She slips it in her jacket pocket.

"Morning, Mel."

"Morning Charlie."

Parked across the road about a half-a-block down the street is a grey late model Ford Escape with Kevin Mark behind the wheel and Milo McTavish in the passenger seat. Milo points a high-powered directional mic at Thompson and Melinda while Kevin takes a series of images with a digital Hasselblad outfitted with a 300mm f/4.5 telephoto lens "Can you pick anything up?"

Milo adjusts the sound on his headset. "Just snippets… there's a lot of interference. Thompson is asking her about Harry, but it's garbled."

It's hard to tell but Melinda seems to object to what Thompson is telling her. It appears as if Thompson is threatening his former colleague. Milo looks at Kevin, "What the fuck is going on?" Kevin shrugs, "How the hell should I know, you're the one listening."

Thompson and Melinda finish their animated conversation. Melinda is pissed. She gets in her car and heads for Quandary's new headquarters above The Smoke Shop restaurant. Milo and Kevin duck down so Melinda doesn't spot them watching. Thompson stands in front of Melinda's building as if he's waiting to be picked up.

A black limo with Chinese Embassy plates drives by. Milo turns to Kevin who's already put down the camera and started the engine. "Get some shots!" Kevin fumbles with the camera dropping the lens cap. He searches for it on the seat between his legs. Milo grabs the camera out of Kevin's hands while Thompson gets in the limo and drives towards them. "Duck!" Kevin looks embarrassed. "Did you get a shot."

Milo is frustrated. "Nah… I was too late, but that limo was definitely a Chinese Embassy car."

Milo looks at Kevin, "What the hell's the matter with you. Follow them." Kevin makes a u-turn and tries to catch up. A red Land Rover SUV darts out of a side street slamming on its brakes, stopping in the middle of the intersection blocking their car. The driver smiles, shrugs, and slowly drives off. The limo has disappeared from sight. Kevin seems almost relieved, "I guess we lost them." Milo grunts almost to himself, "You think." They head back to Quandary headquarters.

Melinda arrives at The Smoke Shop parking lot, but instead of going up to Quandary's new offices, she heads for Harry's flat. She notices the door is unlocked. She walks in; goes directly to the George Condo hanging on the wall in the living room and places the bug Thompson gave her on the inside back of the picture frame.

She turns towards the couch; she takes a Sig Sauer Compact Pistol out of her purse and stuffs it between the seat cushions; she looks up. A handsome young man in a nice suit and open neck white shirt holding a hammer stands watching her. It's Billy. "Can I help you?"

"Aah... The door was open so I thought Harry was home. I'm a friend. I left my mobile here the other night. You know how it is, a couple of drinks and you begin to *lose the plot*."

"I'll help you look."

"That won't be necessary. I found it." Melinda takes her phone out of her jacket pocket and waves it in the air. "You are?"

"Billy. I manage the gallery."

"Oh. I must drop by. I really do need something for my walls."

"Who shall I say came by?"

"Be a darling, Billy, don't tell Harry I was here. He'll think me *a right charlie.*" She rushes past him through the door and out. Billy locks the door behind her. He moves to the couch and reaches down between the cushions. He pulls out the Sig Sauer. He takes out his phone and dials.

"I'm not available. Leave a message."

"Boss, it's me. An attractive well-dressed woman came into your flat while I was installing the *mezuzot.* She was messing with the George Condo and stuffed a gun in-between the cushions of your couch. She said she was here the other night and was looking for her phone."

Caught In The Web

I feel my phone vibrate in my pocket but I let it go to message. I check. It's from Billy, probably some gallery business. I need to think. Roger already left our meeting and was headed for Vauxhall Cross to report to our masters while I made my way back to Quandary's new digs.

I still didn't feel like I was part of the group, not really. Everyone is polite for all that meant, but Roger made it clear that I was his boy, his Number One, free to follow my instincts. That could have gone down like a pint of flat ale, especially for Kevin, who obviously felt senior to everyone else in the group and maybe Melinda, the lawyer. Solicitors always think they're the smartest ones in any room.

Roger did his best to warn the others from initiating any bureaucratic infighting or attempts at empire-building, but working for the government always ends-up producing its share of Machiavellian *tossers*. I listened to Billy's message. The warning seems to have fallen on deaf ears for at least one of my two new female associates. Billy's description pointed the finger at Melinda, a Five interloper, who appears to be weaving a deadly spider's web right under my nose.

"Close and dangerous," that's what Guozhi said. Melinda Byrne, MI5 lawyer, looked like she was still working for, or with, Charlie Thompson. Did she know Thompson was a Chinese agent? Was Thompson running her as part of his network or was she merely attempting to prove her loyalty to Five where her career aspirations seemed to be? Messing with the painting probably meant a new bug, but the Sig Sauer suggested a more ominous intent.

I decide to check in with Billy before I go to the office. Billy is in the gallery supervising the hanging of a new show being installed by the artist. I check the phone Harriet sent me; I can see Billy finished installing all the *mezuzot*. After speaking with Billy it's clear, Melinda was the uninvited visitor. I go up to my flat and check for the bug installed on the George Condo. It's hidden on the inside of the frame.

I go to the couch and pull out the gun. I stare at it for a while, not quite sure what to do with it. Was it there for future use, or was it planted as evidence of a crime I didn't commit? I get too close to the truth and all Thompson needs to do is have an anonymous informant call the cops? The smart thing to do is remove it, but that would tip my hand. I decide to leave it in place but remove the bullets. I wipe my fingerprints.

I call the Quandary office. Milo answers. I tell him to meet me outside the gallery and bring an RF detector. "And don't tell the others where you're going or what you're doing."

I go downstairs and wait a few minutes. Milo finally shows up. "You bring the bug finder?"

"Yes. What's up?"

"How well do you know Melinda?"

"Melinda?" He pauses as if he wants to tell me something but isn't sure if he should.

"Spill it, Milo. Tell me what you know. Someone is fucking with my flat."

"Roger had Kevin and me tail her. She's MI5 you know, and nobody trusts her. She's reporting all our moves to her old gaffer, Charlie Thompson. She met him this morning and he slipped her something. Whatever he told her to do, she wasn't happy about it."

"The other night when everyone was at my flat, somebody planted a bug. Was it her"

"I didn't see her do it. Where did you find it."

"Under the Rosewood bar. I assume one of the group did it when you all were getting drinks."

"It could have been any of us. Jesus, Harry, you don't think it was me, do you?"

"You wouldn't be standing here if I did."

"You think Melinda is the spider?"

"She planted another bug behind my George Condo and she stuffed a loaded gun in my couch."

"What's a George Condo."

"The painting in my living room."

"Cheeky bitch, what she up to?"

"What I'm telling you remains between us." Milo nods. "Charlie Thompson is MSS. He's working for Yang Bo."

"Does Roger know?"

"Yes."

"You want me to check your place to see if there are any more devices hidden?

I fill Milo in on the *mezuzot* and tell him to leave all the devices in place but to give me a list so I know where they are. I then head for the Quandary office and Milo heads for my flat.

Sex, Spies, and Murder

Roger, Milo, and I go for dinner and review the day's events. We discuss how it appears Melinda is a mole planted in Quandary to report back to Charlie Thompson so he can inform Five what we're doing, or inform the Chinese of how close we're getting to shutting down their network.

Milo suggests we not tell Kevin despite his seniority. He describes how Kevin screwed-up the surveillance and how he almost seemed relieved when the red Land Rover cut them off, letting Charlie disappear with his MSS masters. This new Kevin concern is troubling. If he is part of Yang Bo's network, he didn't seem concerned about protecting Melinda, but he also didn't have much choice with Milo sitting right beside him.

Roger suggested that Kevin might have reached his expiry date as a viable agent. "The time comes when each of us has to look in the mirror and say, 'enough'. Perhaps that time has come for Kevin Mark." We agree we have to keep a close eye on both Melinda and Kevin. We finish our dinner and go our separate ways.

On arriving home, I put the television on, hoping to find some mental release from the ever-increasing pressure of having everything I say monitored by Charlie Thompson and his Chinese pals. That release comes in an unexpected visitor.

There's a knock on my door. Someone has by-passed the building security. Maybe it's Billy. I check the phone Harriet provided to keep sur-veillance on my flat. The visitor is Melinda. I look at my couch, trying to decide if I should remove the Sig Sauer. I decide not to bother. It's not loaded and might reveal her intent without caus-ing terminal damage. I open the door. She grabs me by the collar and drags me into the hallway, She kisses me hard, desperate and needy, like someone in need of a sexual fix. When she finish-es exploring my tonsils, she puts her lips to my ear. "Don't say a fucking word. Your place is bugged. They can hear everything you say."

My hands go to her neck. I wheel her around and push her hard against the wall. I run my hands over her body in search of anything sharp and deadly. Her eyes are as big as saucers. She's breathing hard, my hands find her thighs and probe for anything that can damage me beyond repair, but the carnal instinct of two desperate animals takes over. The next forty minutes are a blur. Somehow we end up in bed, naked, sweaty, and exhausted in a tangle of sheets and torn clothing. What transpired felt more like a mid-dleweight mixed martial arts sparring session than sex. Not a word was spoken.

She lay resting, the length of her spent body against mine. Perhaps this is what the songwrit-ers meant when they coined the lyric, "killing me softly." I admit I felt good and guilty at the same time. I was sure Harriet wouldn't mind, but Mercury might not be so understanding. We hear noises coming from the living room. She looks at me. I put my finger to her lips. I lean over and take the Beretta out of the bedside table and slip it under the cotton sheet that partially covers our bodies. I check Harriet's camera phone app.

There's a tall male figure removing the bug from the George Condo. The man moves to the bar and removes the bug from under the rosewood bar. He makes his way to the couch, stubbing his toe on my bronze and glass coffee table. He stifles an expletive. He removes the Sig Sauer from where Melinda hid it. Her eyes meet mine. I feel her body trembling, silently pleading her case for her misguided involvement. She's afraid of me as much as she is of the intruder.

The intruder tip-toes around the opaque high glass brick divider that separates the living area from the bedroom. The gun and his arm appear first, followed by the rest of his body. Melinda pushes closer. She doesn't know I removed the bullets. The tall dark figure aims and fires, but nothing happens, just the click of the coming conclusion. It's the last sound Kevin Mark ever hears. I pull the trigger on the Beretta. Kevin Mark is propelled backward; blood splatters my over-priced glass brick wall. Melinda separates herself from me, grabs my shirt, and puts it on.

She jumps out of bed and inspects our dead ex-colleague. "The gun didn't fire?"

"I unloaded it."

"But how did you know?"

"Billy was watching you when you put it in place."

"I knew something was fishy with this whole Charlie Thompson arrangement, that's why I came here tonight... to warn you, but we got distracted."

"That's not exactly how I would put it, but I get your point."

"Harry, I didn't know. You got to believe me. Charlie told me you were the mole and Roger was running you for the Chinese. He threatened to tell Five I was working with you if I didn't co-operate and help him bring you down."

"So why did you come to warn me?"

"I don't know. It just didn't feel right. Instinct, I guess. I checked you out, and it seemed like you are the last guy in this cluster-fuck of an operation that would be a traitor. It made no sense."

"Well, you're right, Charlie Thompson is the mole and he's been running Kevin for Yang Bo, the Chinese Minister of Science and Technology."

"I wouldn't put anything past Charlie, but Kevin was close to retirement."

"Exactly. He spent his life in service to the Crown, and he never reached the heights he felt he deserved. Frustrated, angry, and disappointed with his life, he decided to cash out with a Chinese dividend. Guys like Charlie Thompson can smell weakness, that's how he's been able to survive as a traitor for so long."

"What are you going to tell the others about me."

"Roger and Milo know what you did, we just didn't know why. Milo suspected something was up with Kevin. I see no reason to tell the others."

"I suppose I'm finished."

"I'll fix it with Roger. We all make mistakes. You were just following your boss's orders. You thought I was the mole."

"Aah... Just one more thing. If you knew the gun wasn't loaded. Why did you shoot?" I don't bother answering. I just toss her on the bed.

"Shouldn't we call Roger?"

"Kevin isn't going anywhere."

Moving On

After Melinda and I finally finish resolving the residual tension caused by Kevin's uninvited visit, I call Roger, who shows up with the rest of the crew. The plan to keep the Charlie-Kevin-Yang Bo cabal confined to those that need to know appears to be abandoned, but Roger is correct, Quandary can't fulfill its prescribed brief if the remaining cast-of-characters didn't have access to the entire script.

Roger instructs Edward and Graham to call the police anonymously but not until they dump Kevin's carcass in a predictable location somewhere off the Canary Wharf. With the disposal organized, he then calls a friendly Copper Supremo, paving the way for a quiet coverup with national security the catchall justification.

Darlene and Melinda are assigned to clean up the blood, but after some rather forceful feminist grousing, Milo is added as the mop-and-pail man under their command. We know from Milo's scan of the other day that there were only two MSS bugs: the one planted behind the George Condo by Melinda and the other planted by Kevin under the rosewood bar. Milo wisely avoids telling anyone about the *mezuzot* cameras I had Billy install.

Roger and I sit in the living room discussing our next move. To be honest, I am a bit surprised at the way Roger is treating me. We have a history of animosity and distrust, and let's not forget, I did appropriate his expensive Graf von Faber-Castell. That may sound trivial to you, but you have to be a pen-person to understand. Besides, Roger did fuck-me-about rather shamelessly in the past. In my defence, I thought he was a Philby clone, and I did set him up for a couple of murders. Needless to say, we have a history. It seems that our conjoined past has resulted in some kind of secret-agent fellowship that the remaining members of our band don't have. Things being what they are, I might consider giving Roger back his pen. On second thought, Roger can buy himself a fucking new writing instrument.

Back to the business at hand; Charlie Thompson will need to do some quick calculations once he learns of Kevin's unscheduled retirement. We don't know if he had someone follow Melinda to my place, necessitating a quick decision to eliminate us, or if the order came from Yang Bo trying to salvage what he could by eliminating unruly impediments. Other than having the government declare, Yang Bo, *personae non grata*, there is little that could be done to a high profile government official like Yang, although I did have some ideas about his daughter Yang Hu, aka Girolama Spera. Her deadly actions necessitate she must suffer her richly deserved *just desserts*. And when I say *just desserts*, I reference both the tasty and literary meanings, with *desserts* referring to its original archaic version *deserts*, meaning entitled reward. Then there's the problem of what to do about Charlie Thompson, the deadly spider forever weaving his sinister web of lies and traitorous conduct: the proverbial Fifth Man.

If history teaches us anything, a notion that is highly debatable, we know traitors don't always get their comeuppance, especially the British ones. None of the Cambridge Five were ever properly punished, Burgess, MacLean, and Philby all defected to the Soviet Union while Blunt and Cairncross basically walked away. Blunt did lose his knighthood and Cairncross lost his job, but neither consequence is a punishment commensurate with their crimes and the damage inflicted on colleagues and country. There are those that maintain that Cairncross wasn't even part of the group, and if so, the Fifth Man escaped not only punishment but detection as well.

Roger okayed my plan to remove Girolama Spera from the world of the living, a suitable penalty for the murder of Jimmy Cotton. She is also believed to be responsible for D. D. Greyson's final exit, but it's the Cotton killing that ultimately determined her fate.

With the house cleaning complete it's time to implement the Spera plan, code-named Mozart's Dessert. Darlene is the only one of the group with an Italian background. I ask if she can cook, she laughs, "I'm Italian, what do you think?"

I remember reading in Spera's file that she's allergic to chocolate. I give Darlene specific instructions on what I need, a list of ingredients that includes amongst other things, arsenic, lead, belladonna, ricotta cheese, semisweet chocolate chips, and a bottle of the best Moscato di Pantelleria she can find.

Melinda and Milo are assigned to keep an eye on Charlie Thompson while Edward and Graham are ordered back to headquarters to monitor and coordinate everyone's activity, once their disposal run is complete. Roger had to report back to our masters at Vauxhall Cross, after which, he figured it would serve us well if he tailed Yang Bo. As for me, I thought a surprise visit to my pal, Yang Guozhi, might result in some useful intelligence.

A Hospital Visit

Yang Guozhi presents an interesting dilemma; he is both enemy and friend; as a consequence, whatever he says or does must always be taken with a grain of rice. A discreet tail seems to be my best option for acquiring useful intelligence.

After about three hours of drinking coffee in a café across the street from the Chinese Embassy, I spot Guozhi's limo pull-up in front and wait, giving me time to get to my car parked a half-a-block away on Broadway.

Guozhi exits his office and gets into the limo. I follow at a discreet distance. Before I know it, his limo pulls up in front of the Harley-Devonshire Clinic, a private hospital specializing in serving those with deep enough pockets to avoid the in-convenience of mudding their Northampton brogues with plebeian dirt. Guozhi enters the stone and brick building alone. He is not a young man so visiting a private clinic is not something that you'd deem unusual. I park my car and follow him, attempting to avoid the waiting limo parked illegally out front of the main building.

My prey takes the elevator to the third floor. I take the stairs. As I open the stairwell door, I spot Guozhi enter Room 307. A Chinese heavy stands guard, arms-crossed, like a Foo dog manning the temple gates. The bulge in his jacket suggests the occupant of the room is someone who needs protection. I approach the counter and ask the young nurse commanding the post as to who occupies Room 307. Her name tag tells me she is Nurse Carman. She declines to answer due to patient privacy protocols. Her manner is formal and stiff until I show her my unofficial DCI credentials.

She hesitates. I can see she is torn as to the right thing to do. "Under normal circumstances, your privacy concerns would be quite commendable, however, these are not normal circumstances."

I lean over the counter so our faces are only inches apart. The act is slightly more conspiratorial than intimidating. "I understand your patients sometimes, how shall I put it, require anonymity, but that said, I am sure your board would appreciate how you protected them from the embarrassment, and perhaps legal liability, of harbouring..."

I pause to let the impact of my words take effect. I turn my head and look at the MSS agent guarding room 307. She follows my gaze. I turn back to look her in the eye, "...a Chinese spy." Carol Reed would be proud of my performance. Nurse Carman rubs her chin as if it might help bring some clarity to her situation. She makes a decision.

"As I said, it is against hospital policy to give out that kind of information." As she speaks she rifles through a series of standing hanging files on her desk. She finds what she's looking for and places it on the counter in front of me. She keeps her finger on the file. "I could get fired if I gave out that kind of information, even to a rather cute copper." She removes her hand from the folder and turns away pretending to busy herself with some papers. I flip open the file.

The report lists the patient as one, David Dennis, and his condition is not good. He has a severely fractured leg, a broken arm, a concussion, and multiple internal injuries. He is a mess. It's almost as if he was hit by a carefully aimed Mini Cooper that drove him through a café window.

I thank Nurse Carman for her discretion. She winks, "For what? I didn't do anything. There's nothing I can do about policy."

I decide to make sure my suspicions are correct. I wander off to the waiting area and position myself with a clear view of Room 307. I watch and wait occasionally scanning several woman's magazines that all seem to be filled with articles on weight loss and tips on pleasing your man. It seems clear the editors missed the memo that we now live in the age of sexual equality where everyone is accepted for their looks and inadequacies. After about five minutes Guozhi leaves.

I approach the door to Room 307. The *shishi* guard sticks out his arm blocking my way. I flash my Detective Chief Inspector ID. I remove his arm. He grabs me. I make a sweeping circular motion with my arm knocking his hand from my shoulder. I finish by smashing his head hard against the hospital wall. "Assaulting a police officer is contrary to section 89 of the Police Act of 1996. If convicted, and I guarantee you would be, you could face six months imprisonment and/or a fine of up to five thousand quid. So I suggest you fuck-off right quick."

I spot Nurse Carman watching closely. I can tell he's about to claim diplomatic immunity, but I cut him off. "You want me to call my close friend, Yang Guozhi, your boss, and tell him you're standing in my way?" He finally backs off.

I enter the room and confirm the identity of David Dennis; he is what's left of D. D. Greyson. He is conscious, but in no condition to talk. I doubt he even recognizes me. It appears D. D. Greyson was working for Yang Guozhi as well as Yang Bo. The most obvious scenario is Guozhi found out about his brother's plan and threatened to expose Greyson if he didn't spy on his brother, but Charlie Thompson was tailing him.

When Thompson found out Greyson was talking to Guozhi, Bo ordered his daughter to poison him, but Greyson had a stronger constitution than poor Jimmy Cotton. Greyson refused to die. He knew Yang Hu poisoned Cotton, so when he started to feel sick, he knew the end was near. He must have gone to Guozhi for help, but the poison had already done most of its work. Greyson thought he was a dead man walking. All he could do was exact vengeance, which worked quite nicely for my old pal, Guozhi.

It seems Guozhi told Greyson to expose his brother's plan to me, not knowing Thompson had Greyson under surveillance. When Greyson sat down across the table from me, either Yang Bo or Charlie Thompson ordered Greyson to be eliminated by a more direct means. Unfortunately for Bo, Greyson survived. If he recovered, he could be used by Guozhi to control his troublesome brother. Once the D. D. thread was pulled, the whole intricate *cheongsam* unravelled.

As I leave the building I notice Guozhi's limo is still parked in front. The back window rolls down. Guozhi motions for me to join him.

Girolama Spera's Just Desserts
Leave The Wine, Take The Cannolis

I am aware, this reflective recounting of events is supposed to answer questions and provide information, however, a recitation of mere facts doesn't adequately supply the subtext needed to justify the sequence of events that is about to take place. I'm never quite sure who gets to read these reports, if anybody, but if you've been fated with the task of reviewing my previous contemporaneous meanderings, you should by now be familiar with my occasional detours into the bureaucratic irrelevant, but nonetheless, morally significant aspects of things. I provide my rationale whether it is wanted or not, despite the knowledge my function does not include second-guessing or moral inertia. Navel-gazing should be left to the supermarket shoppers who leave their carts blocking the middle of the aisle, while vacantly staring at the selection of canned peas that are all the same.

I've always tried to live by some semblance of a moral code. I think semblance is the right term to use since the word implies 'the appearance of a thing' rather than the thing itself. Killing is by any definition an immoral act, but so-called civilized societies do it all the time. We kill to punish, to protect, to survive, and to gain an advantage.

We are by nature violent creatures. Despite my self-deluded fantasy of aesthetic, intellectual, and moral superiority, I too am capable of the most villainous acts. I've killed before; I killed The Beautiful Rat, a traitor that tried to kill me twice, and I threw Arno Koch, an ex-Stasi Mengele clone, out a second-story window.

I am a killer, despite any pretence of moral justification. Is killing Yang Hu, the right thing to do? She killed Jimmy Cotton, and she did her best to do the same to D. D. Greyson, who may yet succumb to his substantial injuries. Greyson is a traitor and perhaps deserves his fate, but who among us has the right to make that decision. Even if he doesn't die, he'll never be the same as he was. So I ask you, is it right to kill the artist known as Girolama Spera, a pseudonym that is evidence in and of itself of her guilt? Yet, it remains a dilemma, a moral quandary, a question of conscience wrapped in a conundrum of doubt.

Fuck-it, I'm killing the bitch.

I pull up in front of Spera's flat with a bottle of Moscato di Pantelleria and a box of Darlene's homemade cannolis. My mobile buzzes, it's Billy, "Boss, I just got a series of calls from the storage companies where you had me rent lockers. They've all been broken into. My guess, it's someone who drives a red Land Rover."

"Maybe you should lock up early. Take a week off and go someplace in the country."

"Nah… I don't like the country. I'm not a landscape lover, but you wouldn't happen to have a spare Beretta hanging around would you?"

"I've got a better idea. I'll send someone over to help keep an eye on things." I hang up and call the office. Roger answers. "Quandary Research."

"It's me, someone broke into the storage lockers I set up as decoys. I need you to send someone over to the gallery to keep an eye on things. I don't want Billy caught in the middle of this."

"No problem, I'll have one of the boys keep Billy company. Seems those paintings may be more than a method of laundering payoffs."

"You should know, Greyson is still alive. Guozhi has him hidden away in the Harley-Devonshire Clinic with one of his men standing guard."

"Did you speak to him?"

"He's in no condition to talk, but I did speak with Guozhi. He warned me his brother would go after the paintings but he didn't tell me why."

"I'll have Guozhi's man removed and replaced with one of ours. Our Chinese friend won't like it but that's too bad. He should have told us."

"It should be someone from Quandary and not the Circus or Five. It Greyson ever gets to the point he can talk, we need to know why the Chinese still need the paintings."

"Have you delivered the present"

"I'm about to do it now."

"Come back to the office when it's done."

I hang up and head for Yang Hu's flat.

She answers the door without much enthusiasm. Hu sees me, turns, and goes back to carefully guiding paint across a large canvas filled with a rather nice charcoal sketch. I close the door and stand over her shoulder in as much as an irritating manner as I can muster. She doesn't react. "How's *Baba*?

"My Father is fine, thank you. You can see I'm busy, so tell me what you want?" I don't respond.

She turns abruptly brandishing a rather large palette knife loaded with Quinacridone Red. "Perhaps you enjoyed feeling me up so much the last time you were here, you want to do it again?" She turns back to her painting.

"That was rather pleasant wasn't it? But in my defence you were carrying a rather nasty blade, so sadly no, that's not my intent. I've come to apologize, make amends, and hopefully lay the foundation for a diplomatic detente."

She turns back to face me. The look on her face is amused. "What kind of game are you playing at? I'm not stupid and neither are you; you know I can't be turned."

I hold up the bottle of Moscato and the box of Darlene's cannolis, "I bring a peace offering. Let's crack this sucker open and share a pastry or two while we discuss the advantages of a mutual non-aggression pact."

She puts down her palette knife, wipes her hands on a rag, and moves to the couch. She plops down on the sofa, arms spread wide along the back. She crosses her legs. "What's in the box?"

"Cannolis." I make my way to the open galley kitchen, find a corkscrew, glasses, and plates.

"What makes you think I like cannolis?"

"Who doesn't like cannolis? Besides, you did pick an Italian *nom de plume* for your creative endeavours." She points to a chair that strategically puts her glass coffee table between us. I open the wine and pour two glasses. There are four cannolis in the box: two are plain but laced with Aqua Tofana and two are filled with chocolate chips. I give her the one with chocolate chips. She looks at the offering and switches both the wine and the cannolis. She looks at me, "You first."

I take a large bite of Darlene's homemade chocolate chip cannoli and a healthy swig of sixty-five pound Moscato wine. I raise my glass towards her, "*Ganbei,*" and take another sip.

"Okay, you're not trying to poison me. Tell me what you want?" She takes a tentative sip of wine and a bite of the cannoli. "You already have a dialogue with my Uncle. What do you need me for?"

"Your Uncle represents certain elements in the Chinese government. Your father represents an alternative group. It might be in everyone's interest if we were able to have a working dialogue with both parties."

"Tell me what you did with my paintings?"

"What makes you think I have them?"

"The decoy storage lockers were a cute idea, but I need those paintings. That's how I make a living."

"You mean *Baba* doesn't pay your way."

"Give me back my paintings and perhaps we can do business."

"You want to tell me why those paintings are so important? Your whole paintings-for-money-for-information scheme has fallen apart."

"They are my paintings, you stole them."

"I do have connections in the art business. Perhaps I can sell them for you." I don't know why I said that. It just came out.

She looks at me with a slight conspiratorial look on her face. She doesn't respond, maybe she thinks that I'm angling to become a double. I can see the wheels in her asymmetrically attractive head grinding hard. Now she has to report back to Daddy. I can't help but feel a pang of conscience. Do I really want to kill this woman? It's too late, the cannolis are already doing their dirty work.

We continue talking, eating and drinking for an hour. It doesn't take long for Hu to polish off both plain cannolis and half a bottle of wine. I leave one chocolate cannoli uneaten. I can see from her increasing discomfort that the Aqua Tofana in the plain cannolis is starting to take effect. She tries to hide her discomfort. "I'll talk to my father and see what he says. Now if you don't mind I'd like to get back to work."

I get up to leave.

She doesn't move. "You can show yourself out. Leave the wine, take the cannoli." The ghost of Fat Clemenza makes his exit.

Two days later Hu is in the hospital struggling for her life. I consider calling Guozhi to tell him what I did but after some soul-searching self-debate, I decide to leave things as they are. Informing on myself may result in retribution for me and others on the Quandary team. I had no right to endanger my colleagues. I just had to learn to live with what I've done and the pangs of self-doubt it creates. It has become clear to me that the life of an agent is filled with ever-escalating moral dilemmas. It is the job and I must live with it.

I confess to Roger that I almost told Guozhi about his niece, hoping, I think, he'd sack me on the spot. He doesn't. He just smiles, "Well, of course, you wanted to, dear boy. You've always been a bit of a boy scout. Not to worry, one way or another, her spying days are done, so in the end, mission accomplished."

I look at Roger, "Isn't that what Bush said?"

A Spy's Frame
More than Meets The Eye

The fact Yang Hu lay in the hospital served little purpose other than eliminating an already compromised player from the field of play. Her poisoning by Aqua Tofana laced cannoli seemed the most appropriate means of retribution, signalling Yang Bo, and perhaps even Beijing, that our tolerance for domestic incursions has reached its limit. Actions have consequences.

Two items remain on our todo list: Charlie Thompson, and finding the true purpose of Girolama Spera's paintings. As far as Charlie Thompson is concerned, word came down from our ringmasters at the Vauxhall Cross Big Top to surveil only. Leaving Thompson in place creates a danger, but it also provides an opportunity to learn more about our Chinese friends' operation. Edward and Graham are tasked with the job.

Roger warns each of us to start taking Milo's silly cryptonyms seriously when communicating. To date, none of us had paid much attention to them, but with bodies beginning to pile up, it seemed prudent to start using them. Charlie Thompson is designated, Grim.

As witnessed in my last go-round with the Chinese, dubbed the Lucy's Breath operation, we know secret information can be easily hidden in a painting's pigment, but somehow I feel this is something else. Although the paintings were used as a way to payoff traitors for the information they provided, they eventually ended up in the hands of local Chinese companies. The question is, why? I doubt the final destination of the artwork is merely a matter of convenience to facilitate the payoff.

Perhaps I should take a closer look at the Spera painting I kept as a sample. It currently resides in the storage area of the gallery. I call Billy and have him pull the painting out so we can take a closer look, then I call my friend, Professor Krish Bakshi at the Art Gallery of Ontario, who analyzed the Marcel painting that hid the secret to solving the Lucy's Breath conspiracy.

"Krish, it's Harry."

"Harry, old friend, it's nice to hear from you. Are you back in town?"

"No, I'm still in London, but I was wondering if you could hook me up with someone here, who'd be able to do an Infrared Reflectography examination of a painting."

"Is this one of those deals like the last time?"

"Yes, I'm afraid so."

"There is someone who I've worked with on panels, Professor Donna Phillips. She works at The National Gallery. She's a bit odd, but she knows what she's doing, and she does like a mystery. She's the Agatha Christie of pigment. I'll call her right now and let her know you'll be in touch." I thank, Krish, and we hang up.

The next morning Billy and I arrive at The National Gallery with Girolama Spera's painting in hand. Professor Donna Phillips is a sixty-eight-year-old grandmother with a shock of unruly white hair, a Catherine Hepburn outfit, and a dazzling gold pin that looks like it's been crafted by Paloma Picasso. She is charming, eccentric, and very competent. She wastes no time in getting to work. Unfortunately, the analysis comes up empty. The painting is just a painting. If Professor Phillips was expecting a hidden Francis Bacon under Spera's ode to Richard Lindner, she was disappointed.

Billy and I drive back to the gallery in silence. I have to think. The paintings have some significance but what? Billy breaks the silence, "Boss, what if we're looking in the wrong direction?"

"What do you mean?"

"What if the paintings are a decoy, a misdirection of some kind?"

"Maybe it's not the painting, maybe it's the actual pigment? Maybe it's not normal oil paint?"

"I think the Professor would have spotted something odd about the pigment, but what if it's the canvas? What if there's something about the canvas material that makes it special?"

"Maybe? The only other thing is the frame."

"The frame! That's brilliant. Who's going to bother with the frame. We can tear apart the painting all we want and find nothing. The secret must be hidden in the picture frame."

We rush back to the gallery. We remove the painting from its frame and set it aside. Billy carefully takes the frame apart and there it is.

The bottom piece of moulding has been hollowed out and a small clear plastic tube has been inserted in the cavity. The tube contains a dozen microchips about the size of a grain of rice. If all the paintings in the storage unit have the same number of chips hidden in the frames, it adds up to a lot of chips. Traditionally hacking is done through software that gets installed on servers after they've been manufactured and installed. If the Chinese have figured out how to install hardware hacks during the manufacturing process, that creates a whole new level of trouble. It's time to call in the cyber boffins.

Cracking The Kraken

We know Yang Bo has Charlie Thompson's people trying to locate the artwork and now we know why. I call Roger and set up a meeting at Quandary to discuss what I discovered. I fill Roger in with as much as I know, which isn't much. Next, I call Mercury and have her send me the key to the storage unit so I have it the next day. I could just take a sledgehammer to the lock but a key is less messy. Buying combination locks would have been more convenient, but the hardware salesman convinced me the key locks are more secure.

I still have time before I meet with Roger, so I decide, I might as well make use of it. It's time to turn over Greyson's files. The files are the evidence we need to nail Charlie Thompson to the wall. They also contain the name of the supplier who provided the picture frames for Spera's paintings, the 798 Art Frame Company and the names of the buyers that ultimately ended up with the artworks.

In retrospect, that information might be the most important piece of the puzzle. We now have a lead to trace how the microchips are entering the country and where they are going. The documents will ultimately land on some bigwigs desk, probably the Foreign Secretary, who will most likely call the Director General of the Security

Service on the carpet for employing a scoundrel like Charlie Thompson.

Politicians will always try to cover their asses. Severe scolding and dramatic finger-pointing aside, history indicates Charlie-boy will more than likely receive a tut-tut reprimand, lose his pension, and end up lecturing on cybersecurity at Cambridge or Harvard.

That may be the government's way of handling things but it's certainly not mine. Maybe I felt guilty for poisoning Yang Hu, and to be honest, I did feel a sense of relief when I heard she still has a chance to survive, but Charlie Thompson is a different kettle of pufferfish. He does not engender any sympathy on my part. Perhaps my attitude is mere masculine chauvinism inspired by millennia of male protectiveness toward the so-called weaker sex. Odd, don't you think, that even in a world of "MeTo" and equal rights, one would feel protective of a female alien spy. Despite the fact, Yang Hu, aka Girolama Spera, is a killer, she is also a foreign national working for what she believes is the benefit of her country; the same cannot be said for Charlie Thompson. He is a traitor, pure and simple, and on a more personal level, I haven't forgotten the beating I took on the floor of an unused convention hall kitchen.

If Whitehall wasn't willing to metaphorically hang Charlie Thompson in the public square, then I just might do it myself, but Charlie Thompson now seemed secondary to the sinister microchip business that appeared to be more threatening to national security than the money for tech scheme. Perhaps the money for technology operation was a decoy, or maybe just a collateral byproduct of the microchip plot. Whatever evil chicken or egg came first really doesn't matter, because this Kung Pao is burned.

I arrive at Quandary with the microchips in hand. Roger, Milo, and a newcomer are waiting. The stranger is Leonard Knox; he's been brought in from the National Cyber Security Centre to help determine how the smuggled microchips work and how any previously installed chips can be discovered. Knox is a rather nondescript man of undetermined age. He seems to lack anything that resembles a personality or emotional response. The man could stand naked in the middle of Piccadilly Circus playing a Zeusaphone and nobody would notice.

Knox is on loan from Langley to liaison with the British on developing a NATO version of the American Skyborg Program codenamed, Kraken. Both programs are based on the United States Air Force's Kratos XQ-58A Valkyrie drone, a two million dollar unmanned combat air vehicle, otherwise known as a UCAV.

Skyborg and Kraken are based on the military design ethic of *attritable* utility: a notion where low-cost, reusable, and ultimately expendable inventory replaces ultra-expensive assets that are limited in use because of their high cost.

Valkyrie drones act as low-cost wingmen for top-of-the-line fighters like the eighty-million dollar F-35 and F-15EX. Pilots control the drones so they can overwhelm and confuse the enemy without putting the highly-trained pilots and their expensive aircraft in danger. The drones act like navy destroyer escorts. The two million dollar price per UCAV allows the airforce to produce a much larger inventory of planes creating a cost-effective tactical advantage.

Knox informs us the CIA has learned that the Chinese developed these microchips to be installed on the servers used in the drones allowing remote operators backdoor access. The MSS must have assets in-place where the servers are being assembled, what we thought was just cash-for-tech is actually cash-for-installation.

Once installed, the chips will allow the Chinese to take control of the drones. All of this is explained to us by Knox in a dry, academic tone that belies the critical nature of what he is saying.

The Chinese are playing a very dangerous game. A signal must be sent to Beijing, a clear and decisive message that cannot be mistaken, but a message the world press wouldn't recognize as retribution. Yang Bo must pay a price for upsetting the status quo.

Knox doesn't want to wait for the key to the storage unit. He wants us to send our people to take immediate control of the City Storage facility and the paintings, but I have an alternative idea.

"What if we send Milo and Melinda to keep an eye on the paintings in case Thompson's people figure out where they're hidden. In the meantime, we replace the microchips with fakes, then allow Thompson to find them. We could have someone on our side offer up their location for a payoff. That's something Thompson would understand. Then we can follow the chips to see where they lead. Maybe we can take down the whole operation. Charlie Thompson and Yang Bo aren't the only ones involved in this scheme. The Chinese would not be happy. We already know the names of the companies that ended up with the paintings. We could have Darlene check them out to see who they are and what they do."

I can tell Roger likes the idea, but Knox doesn't respond immediately. "Not a bad idea. Let me make a call." Knox goes off to make his phone call. Fifteen minutes later he comes back. "Okay, I'll have the fakes tomorrow afternoon. They'll look like the real thing but they'll only function as trackers so we can follow where they go and who gets them. We still need to replace the chips and find a plausible candidate to contact Thompson. Someone he'll believe is doing it for the money and not setting him up."

"Billy is the one who found the chips, so we could get Billy to replace them without endangering the operation by bringing in anyone else."

Knox is concerned but Roger likes the idea. "You think Billy might be willing to act as our snitch? He wouldn't even have to lie. He did find the chips and he works for you. He could tell Thompson you're getting richer while he has trouble keeping his finances above water. What do you think? It makes sense he'd know where you hid the paintings, he helped you stash them."

"I don't like putting Billy in that situation, but he'll do it if I ask."

Knox nods agreement, "Ask him, and if he needs an incentive, tell him he can keep the payoff."

Everything is in place for the operation. Darlene is instructed to check out the companies that ultimately purchased the paintings. Milo and Melinda are sent to City Storage to keep an eye on the merchandise. Billy, Knox, and I arrange for the replacement of the Chinese microchips with the American-made fakes.

Billy's Got Game

Darlene's investigation comes up empty. All the clients that Greyson sold paintings to were shell companies. Each business was nothing more than an address in one of those office buildings across London that rent street addresses, mail-drops, and meeting rooms to entrepreneurs that can't afford expensive full-time office space. The paintings were delivered to the fake offices and immediately picked up by a courier service. The delivery company is just a phone number that goes to the Huli Jing Restaurant & Fortune Cookie Company, owned by a known MSS asset.

While Darlene was tracing the movement of the paintings, Billy got to work replacing the microchips. His picture framing experience was essential to the success of the operation. The artworks had to be removed from their frames, then the moulding had to be disassembled so the microchips could be exchanged, and finally, everything had to be put back together so that no one would notice the switch. The whole process took longer than we initially anticipated. Finally, with everything ready, Billy makes the call. Roger, Knox, Milo, and I are all crammed into Billy's office in the gallery. We assume Charlie will have the call's location traced. Milo has set things up so we can record the conversation.

"Charlie Thompson?"

'Speaking."

"I understand you're a collector."

"A collector? A collector of what?"

"Information among other things."

"I think you have the wrong Charles Thompson."

"So you have no interest in purchasing lost art?"

There's a pause on the other end of the line. "Who is this?"

You don't know me, but we do have a mutual acquaintance in the art gallery business."

"Who's the artist?"

"I believe, she's someone you know. Someone who is currently suffering from some unfortunate medical issues."

"How many of her paintings do you have?"

"I have one, but I know where the rest of them are being stored."

"What makes you think I'd be interested?"

"If you're not, I have several potential buyers that would pay handsomely for them. The frames alone are worth the price I'm asking. "

"Are you selling these items or are you acting as a broker for someone else?"

"Listen, these items are hot... very hot. They need to be moved quickly or it may be too late."

"Can we meet?"

"Sure, I'd be happy to meet. I'll even give you one of the paintings as a show of good faith, but I'll need cash for the location of the others."

"How much are we talking about?"

"One million pounds."

"That's a lot of money."

"It's a lot of paintings, but if money is the issue, I could reduce the price if you don't want the frames."

"No, no, I'll need the frames."

"I have other buyers ready to buy, so I need an answer... now!"

"It will take me a day to put the cash together."

"You have twenty-four-hours or the deal is off."

"Okay, it's a deal. Meet me at the Huli Jing Restaurant tomorrow at two o'clock, I'll bring the money but I need you to bring all the merchandise."

"I'll bring one painting, the others will be close-at-hand, but we have to meet someplace neutral, the patio of the Bull and Peacock in Notting Hill." Billy doesn't wait for an answer, he hangs up.

Roger looks at Billy, then at me. "Where have you been hiding this guy?"

Billy smiles at me, but I'm not that happy with putting Billy in harm's way. I give him a hard look, "You'll take the Beretta."

The following day we arrange to have agents posing as customers and staff strategically positioned on the patio of the pub restaurant. Charlie is no fool, he's played this game before. We have to be smart. Roger and Milo take control of all the shop security cameras on the street as well as all the traffic cameras that monitor the busy commercial area.

Thompson shows up with a suitcase that he slides under a table for four on the patio. He positions himself on the curb facing the inside of the pub. Billy will have to sit with the sun in his eyes. I'm watching from a second-story flat across the street. We notice two Chinese couples enter separately and position themselves within close proximity to where Charlie is sitting. Billy enters carrying the painting wrapped in brown paper. He spots Charlie and takes a seat opposite. He leans the painting against the empty chair beside him.

"You're Harry's guy."

"I run the gallery."

"Harry's a rich bugger and a boy scout, I find it hard to believe that he'd be involved in this."

"You're right. He's not. This is my deal and my deal alone. Kind of an early retirement plan."

Roger and I watch and listen to the conversation in amazement. Billy has taken to this high stakes game of chicken like Daniel Negreanu to a game of Texas Hold'em.

"So, you're flying solo? Harry won't be happy."

"Fuck him! He treats me like shit. I'll take the money and disappear. He'll never find me." Charlie doesn't try to dissuade Billy of the presumed consequences of his actions.

"Tell me, why you think these paintings are worth so much money."

"I hear Harry talking. He said the artist is seriously ill and might die. Artists die, the price of their work goes up, especially if each painting is like a box of Crackerjacks, a surprise in every box. And there's a storage locker filled with surprises... like I said, I hear things."

"How do you know the location?"

"I helped Harry hide them. Harry and I exchanged clothes and cars. I had your people running all over London while Harry stashed them in a secret location, but I saw the rental receipt. I know where they were stashed, but they're not there now."

"Where are they?"

"In a rental van parked nearby. So, let's not quibble over a few quid, I know my art and what it's worth... and I know more about Harry's extracurricular business than he thinks I know."

"I need to inspect the artwork."

"And I'll need to inspect the money."

Charlie pushes the suitcase with his foot towards Billy. He undoes the latch and looks inside. The money is stacked in neat bundles held together by elastic bands.

"It's all there." Charlie signals the Chinese couple sitting several tables away. The man comes over and takes the painting while his female companion takes the seat next to Billy. She jams a Glock 17 into Billy's ribs. Charlie smiles at Billy's obvious discomfort. "Just a precaution while we check the merchandise." Fifteen minutes later the man comes back to the table and whispers something in Charlie's ear. Charlie turns to Billy, "It appears the painting is the real deal. You tell me the location of the van and the money is yours."

Billy writes the license plate number of the van on a napkin and slides it across the table. "It's a dark blue Ford parked across the street from The Portobello Cheese Emporium. All the paintings are in the back."

"You understand if the paintings aren't there, we'll find you. It doesn't matter where you go or how hard you try to hide, we'll find and hurt you, and then we'll kill you. Do I make myself clear."

"Absolutely."

"One more thing."

"What's that?"

"The keys to the Ford?"

Billy drops the keys to the Ford on the table.

The End Game

Sir Andrew P. Davidson, KCB, Director General of the Security Service (MI5) sits rather uncomfortably in the office of Sir William Alexander, KCMG, Chief of the Secret Intelligence Service (MI6). Although the Quandary operation is a joint venture under the official rubric of MI5, everyone involved knows, this is an MI6 operation. Davidson isn't happy about the situation, but Alexander couldn't care less, there is too much at stake.

Harriet sits beside Davidson, across from the head of the SIS, staring at the organization's *Semper Occultus* motto, prominently displayed on the edge of Alexander's desk. Harriet smiles to herself at the bureaucratic gamesmanship being played out in front of her, but she manages to maintain a stolid outward appearance. She knows political sparring is par for the intelligence course, but having a beautiful woman present will invariably increase the stakes.

Davidson looks at Alexander, "It's time..." The words hang in the air like a dagger poised to strike. "William, it's time." Alexander looks at Harriet and nods.

Harriet removes her phone from her purse and dials. A man with a Chinese accent answers on the other end, "Hello."

"Good afternoon, my old friend."

"Aah, good afternoon my dear."

"I'm calling to let you know the approval for your grandchildren's scooters has come through."

'Wonderful news. I'm sure it will be a great surprise. I'm very pleased."

"I just want to let you know the original engines have been replaced. You are aware, they were dangerous. We don't want any reckless behaviour to cause an accident, so we exchanged the faulty parts with benign replacements."

"I see... and the originals, where are they?"

"We have them in a safe place, where they can't do any harm."

"Well then, that will have to do."

"One more thing, old friend. Try to limit your grandchildren's scooter activities, we don't want the wrong people getting hurt."

"Understood, my dear." Harriet hangs up. She looks up at Alexander, "It's done."

Han Jian
The Traitor's Sword

The Portobello Cheese Emporium, located on Portobello Road, is half-a-block down the street from the Bull and Peacock. The purple-painted building is a shop that specializes in fine cheeses from across the world. Girolama Spera's paintings are in a Ford cube van parked out front.

Yang Guozhi pushes down the plastic slat of the Venetian blind so he can see the street below from his second-floor vantage point. Two of his men stare ominously at the wife and mother of the shop owner; both are sitting on a hideous floral settee, petrified by the presence of the strange foreigners. Another of Yang's men holds a mobile waiting for his boss to give the order.

Across the street and down a few stores, Roger and Harry position themselves in the second-floor offices of the Radical Tea Company. The location provides a perfect view of the street and the Ford parked out in front of the cheese shop.

A little further down the street, Edward sits behind the wheel of a grey late model minivan with Graham sitting shotgun. Milo and Melinda sit in the back monitoring a bank of computer screens with feeds from every camera on the street, including new ones Milo installed the night before.

In a small diner across the street and a few doors down from the cheese store Yang Bo and two of his bodyguards sit enjoying tea and biscuits while waiting for the exchange to take place.

The Chinese couple that assisted Thompson remains at the Bull and Peacock guarding Billy, while Thompson casually strolls down the street towards the Ford van.

Guozhi watches. As soon as he sees Thompson approach the Ford he speaks, not moving his eyes from the window. "*Xiànzài. Xiànzài zuò!*"

Seconds later four masked members of the infamous *Xīngxīng* moped gang race around the corner in souped-up black Vespa Scooters performing dangerous high-speed wheelies. Each of the four riders wears a black aviator-style jumpsuit tucked into high-top military-style leather boots. Each jumpsuit has a large "Xx" logo, also in black, silkscreened on the back. The leader wears a brightly painted red and gold gorilla-mask while waving a Han Jian sword menacingly in the air.

His four compatriots wear masks that are painted black. Their Han Jian's are strapped to the sheaths on their backs for easy access. The leader races ahead. His three sidekicks ride up onto the sidewalk grabbing mobile phones out of the hands of distracted pedestrians not paying attention to where they're going or what's going on around them. The Chinese couple guarding

Billy decides it is best if they disappear from the scene. Charlie Thompson is on his own.

The London moped gangs are the Chinese equivalent of the Japanese *Bosozoku* that saw their heyday in the early fifties and sixties. *Bosozoku* means *violent speed tribes*. Both groups cause trouble by racing around busy streets breaking traffic laws and stealing phones from pedestrians too busy on their devices to notice the dangerous delinquents approaching from behind.

Charlie Thompson hears the commotion behind him. He turns to see the red and gold masked moped-riding gorilla approaching on the sidewalk at high speed. He's either too surprised or too late to react. The masked gorilla plunges the twenty-eight-inch blade into the heart of Charlie Thompson. The traitor, Charlie Thompson, falls backward onto the pavement with the Han Jian sticking straight up. The four moped murderers race off down the street. Yang Guozhi's man walks out of the Portobello Cheese Emporium, picks up the keys to the Ford van that are still in Charlie Thompson's hand, gets in the van, and drives off. I look at Roger who's mouth is wide open, "What the hell just happened?"

The next day police find four black mopeds, jumpsuits, gorilla masks, and the remains of about twenty framed paintings in a burnt-out pile in a vacant lot on the outskirts of London.

The Yang clan all returned to Beijing. Bo decided his best option was to voluntarily resign as Minister of Science and Technology and retire. Hu remained a painter with no official or unofficial government duties. Guozhi, on the other hand, was made Minister for State Security.

Harriet and I sit staring intently at the George Condo on the wall of my flat. She puts her hand on my leg. "You're like that painting, my love, an odd mix of reality and fantasy mixed into an enigmatic representation of life."

I'm pleased with her analysis. "You are becoming quite the art critic. Perhaps you've learned something from me after all, it is only fair."

She smiles. "Do you love me, Harry?"

"You know how I feel."

"But you love Mercury, don't you?"

"You know I do, but wasn't it you that told me, two things in conflict can both be true."

"Yes, but it does make me melancholy. I despise the feeling. It's not productive."

"No one feels good all the time, and not everything has to be productive."

"Or real?"

"Yes. Or real."

And so life goes on. It's time for me to call Mercury and let her know I'll be returning to Toronto in the next few days. Until next time...

The End

DECEPTION
"I CANNOT FORECAST TO YOU THE ACTION OF RUSSIA. IT IS A RIDDLE, WRAPPED IN A MYSTERY, INSIDE AN ENIGMA; BUT PERHAPS THERE IS A KEY. THAT KEY IS RUSSIAN NATIONAL INTEREST."
- WINSTON CHURCHILL
WRITTEN BY JERRY BADER
ILLUSTRATED BY PAOLA CECCANTONI

DECEPTION

Deception

The world is a dangerous place, and every country has men and women tasked to protect it. These people go by many names: secret agent, intelligence officer, and analyst are just a few. Harry is one such person. He is an analyst. He spends his time reading, researching, and analyzing, followed by writing reports that often never see the light of day.

Harry is well educated with a seemingly important job, but Harry is bored. Bored, because analysts never get to be the hero, never get to order cocktails stirred not shaken, and, never, never, get the girl. Harry is frustrated, frustrated because his superiors told him the report he just spent six months working on is to be tabled, and no, he can't have a field operative to work with to follow up.

Harry has one very dangerous character flaw, he has an imagination, not something the men on the Top Floor appreciate. Harry needs to prove himself; he needs some excitement in his life, and that excitement comes in a deadly package of intrigue and murder that combines something called the *Sister Project* with a Russian master spy, H, K. Kyrsa, code name, the *Beautiful Rat*, and the devastatingly gorgeous Harriet. The question is, is it all just happening in Harry's head, or is there a real plot that needs to be stopped? Is Harry just plain crazy, or are the Russians out to mess with the West one more time? Harry is on his own, not sure who to trust. Are there any good guys in the world of espionage? The only way to find out is to find Kyrsa, the Beautiful Rat. Join Harry in his search for what may not even be real.

DELUSION: LUCY'S BREATH

Delusion: Lucy's Breath

On a chilly November New York City morning in 1953, a scientist working for the CIA on psychotropic mind-control experiments walked off the tenth-floor balcony of the Statler Hotel. He had become increasingly disenchanted with the bizarre and incredibly dangerous work he had been doing in service to national security. Despite the patriotic rationale, the scientist felt his life's work was immoral and most certainly illegal. He wanted out, unfortunately, he knew too much, and knowing too much is a very precarious position to be in if you work for a clandestine operation run by America's very own version of Josef Mengele, the Angel of Death.

The scientist insisted on getting out, and out he got, through the window and off the balcony of the Statler Hotel on that brisk Fall morning in Manhattan. Was suicide his solution for terminating his deal with the devil or did the devil do him in? It's impossible to say. The evidence although in plain sight is murky and blurred by time and the self-preservation of those responsible. I know what you're thinking, not in my America, not in my beloved United States, not in the home of the brave and the land of the free. Unfortunately, it did happen; it's the kind of thing that happens when governments feel an existential threat.

America has a fundamental flaw, an Achilles heel of perspective and attitude; it fails to understand history and its place in it. In the words of philosopher, George Santayana, "Those who cannot remember the past are condemned to repeat it." If you believe it can't happen here, I urge you to take a look at The Wall Street Putsch of 1933, and the name of one of the participants. You might find it informative. It could happen again. America is under siege by a series of existential threats. It's not some crackpot conspiracy theory; it's history. The question I have is: which is more dangerous, the external threat or the internal threat?

For those who cling to Senator Barry Goldwater's Cold War aphorism, "Extremism in defence of liberty is no vice." I urge you to remember the past because if you don't, you will be condemned to a future you did not expect and an existence you will be forced to endure.

What follows could happen, and maybe will happen if you allow extremism to take hold of the levers of power.

The Outlaw Rider
"If you're not prepared to cheat,
you're not prepared to win."

Jesse James, the daughter of a deceased mob-connected rug salesman, becomes a jockey working for the *Hong Mian* triad in order to feed winners to State Senator Samuel Somersby. The Senator is responsible for approving California gaming licenses. To date, only Native CANGV casinos are allowed to have slots. California horse racing will die if they aren't allowed to add slot machines to their venues. Benson Yeung, Dragon Head of the *Hong Mian* triad, and his chief lieutenant, Johnny Luck, have a plan to force Somersby to approve their Native partner's demands for off-reservation gaming licenses. At the center of the plan is a unique white thoroughbred Spirit horse, prized by Native people, appropriately named Medicine Hat.

Dead End
There Are No Good Guys

It all started five years earlier with the murder of Peter Pretty Boy Chen, a low-level soldier for Benson Yeung's Hong Mian triad. Rumor had it that the Guan Yu statue that sat on the old man's desk, the symbol of his Dragon Head status as leader of the Hong Mian, was filled with priceless Pigeon Blood rubies, or at least that's what Peter Pretty Boy Chen thought. Whether he was right or wrong is a tale for another time and another place.

What's significant is, his desire to get his hands on those rubies led to his brains being splattered all over the wall of the Green Dragon Restaurant. Like all classic California mysteries the past is never forgotten or forgiven; it always comes back to raise its ugly head.

Fast forward five years. We first met Jesse James and her associates in *The Outlaw Rider*, when she was a young female jockey making a name for herself on the track and off under the guidance of her mentor, triad big shot, Johnny Luck. Jesse has moved up the Hong Mian ladder and has made herself a major triad player, but the past is never so far behind that it doesn't affect the present. And so *Dead End* begins.

Palermo
A Place To Die

The race took place in picturesque Palermo, Sicily, but this wasn't your typical horse race with rules designed to protect the horses, jockeys, and bettors; this was a Mafia sponsored street race: a blood sport free-for-all more suited for the Coliseum than the back-streets of the scenic Sicilian town. Race promoter, Santos Luzzato, nephew to Nicky The Mushroom Fungo, wanted in on his American Uncle's horse racing connections with the LA triads. The race leads to a series of decisions that end with a suspicious car accident that kills billionaire heiress and racehorse owner, Josephine Somersby Murphy, sister to the Governor of California, Samuel Somersby, a man with Presidential ambitions and ties to Johnny Luck, LA triad big shot.

Love, sex, murder, and racehorses create a toxic mix of intrigue and suspense that drives Luck's protégé, Jesse James, to Sicily, Argentina, England, and Switzerland in her pursuit of the truth. Who killed Josephine Murphy? Was it Luzzato, Nicky Fungo, Murphy's brother, the Governor, or was it someone closer to Jesse.

Palermo, a place to die.

Stone Cold
Between a Stone and a Hard Place

On the surface, Major William Stone (Retired) is merely a rich, English expatriate with a diverse military and financial services background now living in Palermo, Argentina where he runs a small art gallery along with his assistant Margarita Cervantes.

If you scratch the surface, you'll find that Stone was recently the chauffeur for Mrs. Josephine Murphy, heiress to the Murphy Peanut Butter Company, the largest peanut butter manufacturer in the USA, and owner of numerous expensive thoroughbred racehorses. This seemingly incongruous set of circumstances gets even more intriguing when you learn that Stone inherited over one billion dollars when Josephine Murphy died in a tragic, and somewhat questionable, car accident in the hills of Palermo, Sicily leaving Major Stone the bulk of her estate.

After the Murphy estate is settled, Stone disappears to reemerge in Argentina leading a quiet and peaceful life as a wealthy art gallery owner and financier. His good fortune is tempered by the fact he left the love of his life, Jesse James, protégé to gangster Johnny Luck, back in LA.

The problem is, Major William Stone died in the Falkland Islands and the man now assuming his modified identity is disgraced MI6 financial wizard Jacob Conrad. Conrad took the fall for his Vauxhall Cross masters' illegal shenanigans ending up in jail with a lengthy prison term. According to the British newspaper reports, Conrad died in Belmarsh Prison, only to be resurrected by Section Six's cyber boffins as William Stone, international financial consultant living in Hong Kong, where he runs into Charlie Long,

Dragon Head of the Wan Chai and a major rival of the Hong Mian, led by Benson Yeung and Johnny Luck.

Stone Cold dives deep into the back-story of how Jacob Conrad becomes William Stone, why he disappeared leaving Jesse behind, and who'll control the flow of cocaine into the USA. From Hong Kong to Palermo, London, Cacaloxuchitl, Mexico and Los Angeles, this is a tale of secret agents, drug dealers, money launders, and murders, all wrapped in a delicious recipe of greed, envy, cocaine, and peanut butter chilli.

The Aussie Switch
Published By MRPwebmedia

Horse trainers, Davey and Pauly Cisco are looking for a fresh start in Southern California after wearing out their welcome in their native Australia. The Cisco twins are identical in looks but not personality; Pauly, like most horse trainers, pushes the envelope of acceptable practice, while his look-alike brother rips through regulations with regularity and abandon. It didn't take long for the two brothers to hook-up with a couple of conmen: an expert computer hacker who likes e-gaming and a shyster stock promoter on the lookout for eager marks willing to blow their fortunes on a shady horse-betting consortium. The one thing they didn't count on is an associate of Benson Yeung's Hong Mian triad; an ex-South Korean Colonel who operates a crooked international gambling empire. Two corrupt confidence men, unethical twin horse trainers, and doppelgänger thoroughbreds add up to a combustible confluence of confusion, miss-direction, and murder, with tentacles that twist their way through LA, Sidney, Hong Kong, Seoul, and Macau.

Ballet of Bullets
The Game Is Dodging Death
Published By MRPwebmedia

Internet gambling and the expansion of casinos beyond the Nevada State Line have put a financial strain on racetracks. Johnny Luck, Hong Mian triad big shot, and his beautiful blonde ex-jockey protege, Jesse James, are always on the lookout for ways to expand the triad's gambling operation. Back in the fifties and sixties, Jai Alai was a big deal in Florida. Gamblers would fill the *frontons* and drop thousands of dollars betting on Basque athletics competing in a sport that was so dangerous it was referred to as the Ballet of Bullets and The Game Is Dodging Death.

Johnny Luck sees the potential revenue that could be produced by resurrecting the all but dead blood sport. The question is, how to make it popular again? Jesse has the answer. Television. People will bet on anything; they will also watch anything, as witnessed by the plethora of cooking shows that feature ordinary people competing for who can fry the best egg.

If there's a competition, people will bet on who will win. But where there is money, there is corruption; enter the Miami Bettor's Club, run by old Hong Mian rivals Tommy The King Kong and Marco Antonia Suarez, nicknamed *El Astronauta*. In the end, the Ballet of Bullets becomes all too real for the people fighting for control of the gambling revenue generated by the International Jai Alai League.

What's Your Poison?
How Cocktail's Got Their Names
Published By MRPwebmedia

Why do we call mixed alcohol drinks "cocktails"? How do they get their exotic names: names like the Singapore Sling, Screw Driver, the Alamagoozlum, the Angel's Kiss, the Hanky Panky, the Harvey Wallbanger, Sex On The Beach, the Monkey Gland, the Brass Monkey, the Margarita, the Japalac, the Lion's Tail, and many, many more? Who makes up these names, where are they invented, why, and how do you make them? These questions will be answered in *"What's Your Poison?"* by exploring the incidents, people, and places that prompted the creation of these exotic concoctions.

Organized Crime Queens
The Secret World of Female Gangsters

From the bizarre world of female Japanese motorcycle gangs to the historic rise and fall of London's Forty Elephants, the history of female organized crime is both fascinating and strange. These are the stories, both true and legendary of the female crime bosses that broke the mould of feminine gentility. This is The Secret World of Female Gangsters.

Cowboys, Lawmen, & Outlaws

When we think of the Old West, it seems like ancient history, but historically it was yesterday. Many of the characters of the post Civil War Old West lived well into the twentieth century: Bat Masterson died in 1921 and Wyatt Earp didn't pass-on until 1929. Josie Bassett, one of the Wild Bunch girls managed to hang on until 1963 and she only died then because she got kicked in the head by a horse.

History doesn't end with an era, remnants, artifacts, and people overlap. History doesn't stop because technology and style move on.

The future is more likely to look like the film *Brazil* with its jury-rigged conglomeration of antique flotsam and modern-day technological jetsam, than the bright shiny newness of *Star Trek*. Turning history into fantasy is dangerous; it leads to mistaken notions and bad decisions. Maybe it's time to grow up and see the heroes of the Old West, as they really were, cowboys, lawmen, and outlaws.